THE DRAGON'S DEDICATION

PERIDOT DRAGON SHIFTER BROTHERS

MARIE JOHNSTON

LE PUBLISHING

Cricket

I was born and raised in Las Vegas, so I thought I'd be the last girl to say "yes" in an impulsive Vegas wedding. But I met Maverick at a wedding reception, the one where my ex was marrying my boss. I was vulnerable, Maverick was the hottest guy I'd ever seen, and he was nice. Even more, he was interested. I'm sure I won't regret marrying a stranger who can make my toes curl by just looking at me.

Maverick

I saw Cricket, and I wanted her. I knew exactly what she was going through at her ex's wedding since my own ex immediately mated someone else. There's only one issue. Two, really, thanks to Cricket's overprotective brother. My new wife doesn't know I'm not human. I'm a dragon shifter who has to live with his clan—far away from Las Vegas. And Cricket will either have to accept me, or pay the price, while keeping her brother blissfully unaware. I'm sure I won't regret marrying a lovely human I met and had to have.

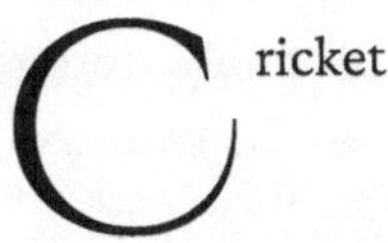

Cricket

THE LIGHTS of the reception hall strobed with the beat of the deafening music, stabbing into my brain until it was as porous as Swiss cheese. I pressed my fingertips to my forehead.

"Are you all right?" my coworker Jill shouted. She nearly tipped off of her stool as she leaned toward me. The drinks were flowing as freely as the tunes.

She'd asked me five other times tonight but for different reasons. The main one being the groom with a deliriously happy look on his face. His bride was my boss, who he'd met while he was dating me.

Ever the good sport, I'd gone to the wedding, and I was suffering at the reception.

"I might have to go!" I shouted back, wincing as the

effort made my brain hurt. Without the emotional strain, I might've made it through the night.

She gave me a pouty look and wrapped her lips around two cocktail straws. Without letting go, she closed her eyes and sashayed to the beat.

I loved music, but not like this. I'd been sensitive to noises my entire life. My parents and my brother had learned what kept me from throwing a tantrum as a kid, and now that I was grown, it was my job to take care of myself before the migraine from hell set in.

I hooked my purse bandolier style over my shoulder and slipped off the stool. The rest of our work crew was on the dance floor, in the bathroom, and a few had snuck downstairs to the casino. Others were probably doing things that would be illegal in other parts of the country, but this was Vegas.

"See you next week!" I tried to smile, but it ended up being a grimace. She waved, and I weaved around tables and chairs on my way out.

I didn't bother to say goodbye to the bride and groom. My boss had no issues at last year's Christmas party flirting with Peterson, my boyfriend of five years, the man I thought I'd marry and have kids with. We'd planned to build a house in Henderson, get a dog, and I was sure he would propose by the Fourth of July.

He had. Just not to me.

Tears burned the backs of my eyes. I was over him—God, I hoped I was over him by now—but I mourned the dream that had been obliterated when he'd broken up with me. I was still raw from hearing my boss gush about the new man she'd started dating with a last name for a first name.

You might know him, Cricket. He was at the Christmas party.

Carrie could have him, how he gassed up after Monday night football and all the wings he shoveled in his mouth.

Black edged my vision as I rounded the last table. The doors were in sight. Going straight for the light at the end of the tunnel, I strode into the open-air area that two other hallways dumped into.

One of the hallways led to the room the wedding ceremony was held in. I veered toward the second hall-way, blinking my eyes and hoping I made it to my hotel room before I started crying. The last thing I wanted anyone to think was that I was shedding any more tears over Peterson.

I slammed into a hard chest and strong arms wrapped around me. The pounding at my temples abated slightly as I focused on the person I'd run into. My heart sank, but my body tingled where he touched me. Just my luck. The most handsome man I'd ever seen witnessed my despera-tion to flee from the reception.

At least I was dressed cutely in a simple emerald-green cocktail dress and my brassy hair was pulled into a sleek bun. Some days, the small wins counted.

"Sorry," I mumbled and tried to get around him. The pain was returning and my spiked adrenaline wasn't helping.

"Are you okay?" His deep voice was almost too sinful for Sin City.

I couldn't bring myself to look at his face and kept my gaze solidly planted on the divot in his neck that was visible between the open collar of his pale-yellow polo.

His hands were still on my shoulders as if he wasn't sure I was steady. I snuck a peek at his eyes. They were stunning. Sharp greenish-yellow eyes bored into me, catching me in a tractor beam. I'd never seen such a bright or intense shade of chartreuse, but then I didn't get out much. Maybe he had special contacts or something.

Dipping my gaze only landed me on his wide chest. The pale yellow of his polo should've been a visual assault after the dark reception hall, but the color was soothing. Perhaps it was the guy?

He ducked his head to look into my eyes and I realized I had never answered his question. Was I okay?

It must be the fact I'd never seen him before, would never cross paths with him again, and that he clearly wasn't a part of the wedding party that made me run my mouth.

"I'm okay as long as you don't consider the fact that my long-term boyfriend from last year just married my boss, and I had to show up and look like I was happy for them, or it would affect my job and for some reason, make *me* look like the poor sport. And I'm getting a migraine, so there's the cherry on top of a really shitty night."

The last few months had been a crap sundae.

A low chuckle vibrated out of his chest, and I wanted to lean my forehead against his warm body and let the heat sink in and chase away the pressure in my skull. I could ask him if I could do that. We were in a casino in Vegas. The simple request wouldn't be that weird.

"My longtime ex just mated—*married*—someone she barely knew. I left town for the week even though my sister's my boss and not my ex's new love." He smirked and leaned down to conspiratorially whisper, "My sister wouldn't have ever asked my ex out."

A chuckle bubbled out of me, and the aura around my vision began to ebb. I'd never experienced diminishing symptoms before. The only way out was through, in my experience. "I thought at the very least I'd get a free dinner, but they only served appetizers and we had to pay for our water at the bar."

His hands were still on my shoulders, and I couldn't bring myself to care. It was like his touch chased away the pain.

"How's that headache?" he asked.

"Waiting in the wings to get terrible. I was trying to escape before it got really bad and people started thinking it was the happy couple getting to me." I rolled my eyes and flinched. The pounding in my brain was ready for its moment to hammer against my skull. "I don't want anyone to think I was distressed because of the groom. He's gotten enough of my time and energy."

His gaze flicked over my shoulder. "Would that be this groom?"

While I was trying to figure out what he meant, a familiar voice came from behind me. "Cricket? Are you leaving already?"

Stiffening, I spun. There was the happy couple, smiling sweetly at me with a touch of concern in their eyes. And wasn't that the rub? They had no idea what they had done wrong. No clue why I would be upset or even less than ecstatic about their happy day. In Peterson's mind, he'd broken up with me before he started seeing someone new, and to my boss Carrie, she cared about little more than herself.

I opened my mouth to speak, but the guy I had run

into answered for me. "I'm afraid Cricket and I stepped out. She's fighting a headache."

Surprise registered in Peterson's expression, like he hadn't noticed the man I was with, or he'd assumed this handsome snack wouldn't be with me. "I don't believe we've met."

Carrie added in her simpering tone, "I didn't realize you had a plus-one, Cricket."

"I..."

"I just got here." My impromptu date stepped forward, hand stuck out. "Maverick Peridot. I didn't want to intrude uninvited, so I told my girl I'd meet her when the dancing started."

Maverick Peridot. I liked it. I liked him and I knew next to nothing about him other than he smelled like vanilla and amber and I felt better around him.

Peterson shook Maverick's hand, his fingers swallowed in a crushing grip. I smothered a snicker. Carrie held her hands in front of her, her fingers twining as she studied my date. Interest lit her eyes, a clue to how long —or how short—the new marriage would last.

Maverick released Peterson's hand and stepped back, snaking an arm around my waist. The throb in my temples ebbed once again. Could I soak up his heat until the pain went away altogether? I had the inclination that he would let me.

Who was this guy?

"Congratulations to the happy couple," Maverick said. "My brother just said his vows with the love of his life." His grin was self-deprecating and utterly devastating. How was it possible a man could look like that and have taken better care of me in five minutes than Peterson had in five years?

"Oh?" Carrie leaned forward like she was trying to get closer to Maverick. "Are you from around here?"

Maverick chuckled, and the sound was better than any Excedrin. "No, the happy couple was so sweet, I had to get away for a while. I'm from Minnesota."

Confusion wrinkled Peterson's brow. "Then how did you and Cricket meet?"

Maverick had been doing so well, but the tightening of his arm around me prompted me to blurt the first thing that came to mind. "Online. I figured there're no good guys in Vegas and I'd have to widen my net."

Carrie tittered. "I'd have to disagree. I found my Peterson right in my backyard."

Of her Henderson mansion. I was there. A catty comment would only make me look like the bad guy. "Well, I hoped having half the country between us would help me get to know the real Maverick. Wouldn't want anyone stealing him away," I said brightly. I couldn't help myself.

A low rumble emanated from Maverick's chest into my side plastered against him. Was he trying not to laugh?

"We've met a couple of times, but I knew after the first meeting she was mine." Maverick's grin was almost predatory and the swirling in my belly liked it a lot. His arm cinched around me, bringing me closer to him. I liked that more. "I'm hoping to talk her into making the move north."

Carrie's lip stuck out. "We'd miss you at work."

Alarm punched the giddiness into submission. Someone like Carrie would have no issues firing me if she thought I was going to ditch the workplace first. I didn't like her, but my stable job kept a roof over my head and prevented my brother from worrying over me like the mother hen he was growing up.

"I wasn't planning on moving anytime soon. I'm not running off to get married right after we just met."

The darkening of Peterson's eyes was the first time I'd seen him acknowledge in some way he'd done me wrong. And he didn't like me pointing it out one bit.

"Good to hear." Carrie's smile was serene and shallow. "I'd hate to learn I'm losing an employee on the happiest day of my life."

"Well," Peterson said as he hooked an arm around his glowing bride. "I hope you can rally and join us. The night is young, and I wouldn't think someone born and raised in Vegas would be so quick to drop."

I bristled. Both his tone and his words were pointed jabs directed toward my weaknesses. He had never taken my migraines seriously, always prodding me to do more than was comfortable and not quite believing the extent of my symptoms. He urged me to go to loud nightclubs on the weekends, even on weeknights, and if I didn't go or had to leave early, he pouted. I started to believe that maybe if I was stronger, I could be the person he thought I was.

Dick.

I flailed for a response and came up empty. My job was on the line if I insulted my boss's new husband, and they'd have no problem blaming me for casting a shadow over their happiest day.

Maverick saved me again. "I'm going to take care of my woman—like a real man should. We'll return if she thinks she's up to it, but if she's not, I have no problem pampering her for the rest of the night."

Carrie clutched her hands in front of her like she was

watching two kittens nuzzle each other. "Aw, that's so sweet. Come on, Petesy, let's return to our party."

She dragged a scowling Peterson away.

Maverick muttered in my ear, his hot breath caressing my skin. "I think my dick just shriveled."

I sputtered, scrambling to hold in my laughter so my boss wouldn't think the joke was about her. "You mean you don't want the nickname Mavsy?"

"My brother calls me Mav sometimes. Definitely not Rick—I'm not a middle-aged man going through a midlife crisis."

"I don't think any woman who watched *The Mummy* in her formative years would equate a frumpy, burned-out dad with Rick."

"Good point. Do you have a nickname? Bug is too easy."

His arm was still around me and neither of us had moved to break apart. I certainly wasn't going to be the first. "My brother calls me bug."

"I'll think of something."

I lost myself in his vivid eyes. "Do you really think we're going to be around each other long enough to think of a nickname?"

"Didn't we just tell the man I was going to take care of your headache so we could go back to dance?"

My whole evening had changed. This morning, if someone had asked me how I thought this night would go, I would've described it exactly up to the point I ran into Maverick. Now I had no idea, but I desperately wanted to find out.

~

MAVERICK

I SAT the cute little human on one of the long benches lining the wall. Tipping her face up to me, I put my thumbs at her temples. "Close your eyes."

I couldn't quit touching this girl, and her impending migraine was the perfect excuse to keep my hands on her soft skin. When she'd barreled into me, I'd barely noticed more than her fresh linen scent. Then she blinked at me with soft-brown eyes edged with pain, and I was hooked. Why was she hurting? Why did she act like everything was normal when her boss and her ex got married? Should I tell her she was the prettiest girl I'd ever seen?

Cricket wasn't sexy in a blatant bombshell way. She had red highlights in her soft-brown hair, warm undertones in her skin, and she was on the shorter side, the top of her head barely reaching my chin. The green dress she wore would seem simple to most men, but that meant they were simple too, too lazy to see the beauty underneath. Her square collar didn't show any cleavage, but the way the material rounded over her breasts and flowed around generous hips to fall just below her knees drove me just as wild. The emerald green she chose affected me on a deeper level. Jewel tones for a gem. At first glance, she could be considered plain. She was anything but.

I couldn't believe the story she told me about the wedding until I met the bride and groom. They seemed shallow enough to have done something so heartless to a person who had a significant role in their lives. How long had Petesy and Cricket been together? Petesy was clearly too wrapped up in his image to know the bride would move on in five years with a new guy who made her feel more powerful, and she'd take half of everything when she went.

To be fair, the bride would likely be justified looking outside the relationship for someone who actually cared about her. Petesy only cared about how she looked on his arm.

Petesy was fucking dense not to see the real jewel he had with Cricket.

I concentrated on easing the pinch of her headache, relaxing the vessels in her head to make the headache a thing of the past. I didn't have the full healing powers of my sister. She was the oldest ruling sibling and therefore was born with healing abilities I doubted she had ever used. But as her twin, I'd gotten some residual powers. My ex used to tease me about being a placebo while my sister was the cure.

For once, the thought of my ex didn't make me want to find another city to disappear into. I was just fine where I was at, with my fingertips brushing against Cricket's satiny skin.

"What are you doing?" she murmured.

"Just a light facial massage. Is it helping?"

Her pink lips pulled into a quick frown. Her lower lip was plumper than the top, and before the night was over, I hoped to know what it was like to rub my thumb over it. "Actually, yes. Just being out of the reception room made my head feel better, but the pounding is almost gone."

I grunted, but really I wanted to pump my fist in the air. "Just close your eyes and relax. We'll have this headache taken care of in no time." Placebo, my ass. I had some healing ability, and it was useful.

She did as I asked, and I used the opportunity to study her even more. She was lovelier than I had first thought. Soft skin with a tiny scar above her left eyebrow. A healed hole in her nose where a piercing used to be. Humans wouldn't be able to detect what had once been there, but I wasn't human. Her chest rose and fell with steady breathing. The slight tension that had been radiating under her skin since she'd first crashed into me dissipated.

She opened her warm-brown eyes, and this close, I could see the smaller flecks of a deep brown. Her right iris had a tiny circle larger than the rest. A birthmark right on her eye. Special, just like I sensed she was.

"It's gone. All the pain is gone." The awe in her voice was the best thing I'd heard all year.

"I'm a male of many talents." Damn, I was getting rusty. I'd screwed up my speech a couple of times tonight, saying mate instead of marriage. Male instead of man. Small errors, but a tiny crack that could lead to more critical mistakes, ones that would threaten my life and hers.

Her lips curved up, and I lost the battle to resist tracing the outline. Her mouth opened slightly as I did.

Warm and soft, just like I thought. I was fondling the human. *Stop it.* "Just making sure you felt better everywhere."

"I can promise you I do."

"Promises in my world aren't made lightly." I held out my hand to help her off the bench. When she was standing and gazing up at me, her attention focused on me just like I selfishly wanted, I continued. "We take our vows very seriously."

Deep yearning flashed in her eyes before she replaced it with humor. "Let's hope the groom takes his more seriously than his promises to me."

"My people would kill him for breaking his promises

to you." Okay, so that was a bigger error in speech. I spoke the truth, but it wasn't something Cricket would understand.

"Your people?" She tilted her head and her gaze brushed over my black hair and my easily tanned skin. I knew what she was wondering.

"My ancestors were Métis, but that's not what I'm talking about. Where I live... we function differently."

"All of Vegas functions differently." She gave a little shrug and a rueful smile played over her lips. Goddamn, she was adorable.

There was no reason for me to stay, but I couldn't bring myself to leave. The bride and groom expected us to enjoy the reception, and dammit, that was what we were going to do. "Now that you feel better, let's dance."

Her eyes flared before I tucked her under my arm and led her toward the ballroom. She stiffened at first, but as we moved, she molded into me. Perfect.

Inside, her tension returned. "You don't have to stay. I don't want to dominate your vacation."

"You saved me from a boring night of wandering the casino to see what else there was besides slot machines and poker tables."

"You should catch one of the shows."

"I don't like any of the singers." I led us through the tables and straight toward the dance floor. It was the only way I could justify continuing to keep my hands on her.

As luck would have it, a slow song was playing. From the corner of my eye, I caught the groom watching us from where he was standing with the bride in a gaggle of women cooing over her dress. His gaze tracked Cricket.

He caught me watching him and started. I made sure my expression said *you missed out and now it's my turn.* I maneuvered us over the floor to the beat of the song while keeping her back toward the happy couple.

Her hand was flared on my back, and I had her other one in my grip. She tipped her face up to me. "What have you done since you've been in town?"

Was she feeling awkward? Was that the reason why our conversation seemed suddenly forced? I was enjoying the quiet cocoon we made among the other dancers. "I wandered through every casino on the Strip, but I can't remember which one is which. They blend together."

"There's more to do than what's on the Strip. You can go to Red Rock Canyon, check out Fremont Street, or take a little drive and see Hoover Dam."

"If only I had a tour guide." I inspected her reaction. I wasn't joking. My trip was over in a few days, and I would make the most of it.

Because this girl was mine.

Tension stole through her body right into my fingertips. "I'm sure there's someone who—"

"What are you doing?"

"Me?" she squeaked.

I was losing her. She was panicking and getting stiffer with each step. I wasn't done with this girl, but I would be if I scared her away. "There's something between us, Chirp."

"Are you trying out chirp for a nickname?"

"It'd be weird if I used the same one as your brother."

Pink dusted across her cheeks. "I haven't come up with anything for you yet."

"That means you need to get to know me better. What do you say?"

We floated across the floor. I was so intent on her answer I didn't notice the bride and groom were now dancing until they bumped into us. I was a dragon shifter; I should've sensed them, but this girl had me acting out of sorts tonight.

Peterson shot an admonishing look toward Cricket as he swirled away with his bride.

Resolve filled Cricket's eyes. "You've got yourself a tour guide."

TWO

ricket

MY HEAD PULSED when I pried open my eyes. Where was I? I licked my lips, tasting the cocktails I'd indulged in last night. The term *liquid courage* had never been so true.

I was on my belly, staring at the far wall of what appeared to be a nice enough hotel room. The only problem was I didn't know what hotel I was in or why.

What happened last night? I sifted through my pickled brain to retrieve any memories possible. Peterson's wedding. The migraine—wait. The migraine hadn't happened. Why?

The man. Maverick. Gorgeous, deep voice, and so damn sweet it was hard to resist him.

Had I resisted him?

With a gasp, I pulled the blankets up to inspect my body. My dress was still on, if twisted and wrinkled.

"We didn't have sex," came that deep, resonating voice that I could record and listen to every night of my life but was so much better in person.

"What time is it?" My words came out thick and raspy. How much had I had to drink?

Too much was the obvious answer.

I twisted to look over my shoulder and there he was. Stretched out on his side, his head propped in his hand, wearing nothing but a pair of boxer briefs. The dark color of the fabric did a poor job of hiding the monster underneath.

He smirked as he answered. "It's almost noon."

I sank into the mattress with a groan. I had the day off, and I'd had the foresight to take Monday off so I could miss the water cooler chatter about how beautiful the wedding was and how amazing the bride and groom looked together, how happy they were going to be. The loving way Peterson doted on Carrie. No thank you.

More of the events at the reception trickled into my brain. Dancing with Maverick. Growing increasingly nervous. He was too good to be true, had to be. Maybe he was a serial killer, and he'd asked me to be his tour guide so he could lure me into the desert and... I'd never been able to finish the scenario. His looks distracted me each time I tried to worst-case scenario my fears. So I'd had a drink. And then another. And another.

And he'd been next to me for each one, cautioning me. If my brother had been there, Vaughn would've told him his words of warning were nothing but a challenge.

You hate to be told what to do, but you need looking after. My brother's words had become a mantra while we were growing up. And look who'd turned out to be right?

I rubbed my hand over my face and stopped. A gold

band twinkled on my left ring finger. "What the hell is that?"

"*That* is a wedding band."

It wasn't that I didn't remember going to a wedding chapel with him. It was supposed to have been a fantasy. A lucid dream. Something I kept locked in my brain. That wild notion true love could be found in an impromptu Vegas wedding. I had accepted the offer to be his tour guide, and then I'd upped the ante. Carrie and Peterson had been making a spectacle of themselves on the dance floor, professing their deep, long-standing love for each other. It'd been months since they met! And then Carrie had been paraded around the ballroom by the groomsmen, guys I'd known for years, who I'd thought would be groomsmen in my wedding. They had ignored me all fucking night. It was as if we had never met when I had been to their houses, sat through their weddings, and given them baby shower gifts. Assholes, all of them.

I hadn't been able to stand it any longer, and I dragged Maverick out of the ballroom. And we had happened across the twenty-four-hour wedding chapel.

My bright idea was staring me right in the face. I knew why I had done something so crazy. What about him?

"Why did you agree to it?"

I flopped over to face him and ignored the throb at my temples. I deserved this headache. Each cocktail I'd poured down my throat was an unspoken admission I knew I'd fucked up.

His gaze was steady, the cut of his jaw stern. How could he be more handsome in the full light of day after a night of partying? "The people in my family have to get married by a certain age. I have some years yet, but last night had seemed like a good time."

"Your excuse is that you *had* to get married," I said flatly. "You don't even know my last name."

"Cricket Kelso. You had to fill out the form in the chapel, remember?" His smirk was gentle. "And I didn't *have* to get married." He rolled closer and I strained back. My ass was about to fall off the bed. "I've never felt like this with someone, Cricket. Never. I wasn't going to just let it go, and I don't have enough time in Vegas to do the whole dating thing."

"We have to get it annulled." It was the only thing that made sense. I couldn't be married. I'd been in one relationship in all my adult years, and that man had dumped me faster than a handful of scorpions as soon as someone else was willing. The breakup had hurt. If I fell for Maverick and he rejected me? It'd be like life proving I shouldn't believe in true love—I don't deserve it.

"How about we just take it one day at a time? You said you have a few days off, and I'll be in town for a few more days."

I scowled at him and rose to a sitting position. I tried to straighten my dress but gave up. My clothing was on and my underwear was riding up my crack. Nothing had been moved, and I didn't pass out from the alcohol. He'd tucked me in and kissed my forehead like he was warding off another migraine. My wedding night, and I got a kiss on the temple.

"We didn't even have sex," I grumbled, knowing full well it would've been a bad idea given the state I'd been in, and Maverick would've been taking advantage of me. I was still grumpy about it. "It doesn't look like you want to be married that bad."

"When I finally get my tongue on that warm little clit between your thighs, you're going to be good and sober."

I broke into a coughing fit by choking on a gasp I didn't know was indignant or a plea for him to do just that. "Okay then."

I went to stand up, but his sudden hard grip on my hips stopped me. "I mean it, Cricket. You begged me to take you, and it was the most painful night of sleep I've ever had, but when we're together, you're going to know who you're with and why."

"Point taken," I said hoarsely. He released me, and I wanted to flip over and roll into that big body of his. I fit neatly into his embrace. He'd already proven that several times last night, on and off the dance floor.

On shaky legs, I rose and stumbled to the bathroom. Inside, I slapped my hands against my cheeks like I was an eight-year-old boy forgotten at home by his family at Christmas. My hair was all over the place. One side was smashed and tangled by the scalp, and the other side was more like the drawing of a child trying to capture my hairdo. My face alternated between pale and flushed, as if my skin couldn't decide whether to be scared soulless or go for plain humiliation.

I glanced at the gold band on my hand. How about both?

When you come to live with me, we'll fit the band with a proper jewel. You can pick from my collection.

Had I imagined Maverick saying those words?

No, I'd gotten drunk, not plastered. Drunk enough to think marrying a stranger was a good idea. Drunk enough to regret my boring accounts manager job and the five years I'd given to Peterson. Drunk enough to think Maverick was as genuine and as sweet as he was panty-dropping gorgeous and not a complete psycho planning to turn my blotchy skin into leather chaps.

Morbid much, Bug? My brother's voice resounding in my head made me gasp. What would I tell Vaughn?

There was a light knock at the door. "Everything all right?"

"Yeah, why?" I covered myself with my arms as if my dress wasn't already doing the job. How had he gotten to the door so fast? Was he going to barge in? It was locked, but all sorts of scenarios were running through my head.

"Just making sure. Yell if you need anything."

An annulment. A way to turn back time. An explanation that wouldn't make my brother roar across town and tear Maverick apart.

Though, to be honest, I wasn't sure my brother could take Maverick. Vaughn was tall and fit too, but Maverick radiated a strength my pediatrician brother didn't.

I shook my head and the dull throb settled in. There would be no fighting. I'd take a few days, figure out what the hell to do about the man on the other side of the door, and then I'd laugh about the ordeal while my brother quietly died inside but ultimately would be okay because I was sitting across from him—alive and well.

Untouched, except for a kiss to my forehead.

Now, I needed to pull myself together. Get some water to chase this headache away. But first, I needed to freshen up. The countertop held nothing but a shaving kit, a comb, toothbrush, and toothpaste. Maverick wasn't one for toiletries. Did he even bother with cologne? After-shave? Body wash?

I peered into the shower. Nothing but the shampoo and conditioner the hotel offered. Where did his decadent vanilla amber smell come from?

So, a shower was out of the question. I didn't like the idea of climbing back into dirty clothing, and I had to spare what was left of the makeup on my face. After using a squirt of his toothpaste on my finger to freshen my mouth, I combed my hair into submission. Yesterday, I'd had an appointment to get my hair professionally styled. The strands were still glossy, but a hint of the frizz was returning. Maybe that was how I could scare Maverick away. Let my natural curls take over, and rub the remaining concealer off my face to reveal my freckles.

I liked my freckles, but since Carrie had once made a comment during one of our team bonding exercises, I hadn't wanted to give her any more ammunition at her reception. *Oh my god, are those the liver spots my mom warned me about?*

I placed my hand on my chest and took a deep breath. Would I walk out of the bathroom and find no one? The whole evening had been a hallucination? The morning could still be a result of too many cocktails but an extension of my delusion.

Walking into the main room obliterated that fantasy. Maverick was very much a real man. And very much shirtless.

A new fantasy ignited.

He was standing over an open black suitcase. The fabric in his hands had to be a shirt. *Please be a top of some sort.* Because the jeans he wore were sinful enough to make me forget his hard pecs and rippled abs were on display.

I swallowed hard, forcing my gaze on his face and those vivid eyes. "Um, so what now?"

He shrugged into a navy-blue pin-striped polo, and I used every ounce of self-control I had to keep from visually gobbling up his torso. "We get something to eat. The real question is—do you want to go out somewhere or order in?"

Staying in a hotel room with this man to eat breakfast —or was it lunch?—wasn't a good idea. For my own sanity, I said, "Out."

~

MAVERICK

I'D GOTTEN myself into a heap of shit, and I couldn't bring myself to care. There was something about Cricket I couldn't resist. And now we were married.

My sister was going to be upset. What will my brother say? Both of them would point out I had made an impulsive decision because of my younger brother, Levi's, recent mating. Maybe they'd be right, but I would remain attached to this little human for however long she would have me. I wouldn't give up on trying to draw her to Minnesota with me, to check out the town I grew up in, and where I was destined to live. Cricket wasn't happy in Vegas. She might think her selfish ex was the reason for her unhappiness, but it wasn't. She wasn't a big city girl.

She was mine, and that meant she was a Peridot Falls girl.

We entered the restaurant on the bottom floor of the casino. Chimes dinged around us. The sheer auditory assault on my heightened hearing the last few days had been hard, but I wouldn't have to endure the onslaught much longer.

Doing my best to block the noise out, I put my hand

on Cricket's lower back and led her toward the hostess stand.

The young girl grabbed a couple of menus and plastered on a bright smile. "Two today?"

Cricket clasped her hands in front of her like she was afraid to touch me. She nodded, and we were led to a small booth along the window facing out to the rest of the casino.

I ignored my menu. "I know we need to talk but hear me out."

She was staring at the colorful plastic in front of her, but her eyes were unfocused. She wasn't reading the list of options. "Okay?"

"You're off today, tomorrow, and the next day. We hang out with each other, day and night—no pressure in the bedroom—and we get to know each other. No major decisions until the last night together." I desperately needed her to say yes. No one at home had to know I'd gotten married in Vegas until I brought a mate with me. When was the last time a dragon shifter married? The ceremony meant nothing to us. We needed a mating ceremony. With our mate. Bonded together for the rest of our lives.

If I returned to Peridot Falls and word got out I had not only gotten hitched in Vegas but had a subsequent annulment, I'd have a hard time getting taken seriously. And since I was in the ruling family, the twin of the actual ruler, I wasn't in a position to get shrugged off. Everyone would look at me with pity in their eyes. The whole town knew my history with Astra, my ex. Everyone knew she had gotten mated within months of our breakup. They also knew my brother had just found the love of his life. They'd assume, rightfully so, dammit, I had gone off the deep end. Succumbed to grief over Astra's mating, or desperation or sheer panic that I wasn't going to mate anyone before my thirty-fifth birthday.

"We need to dissolve this marriage." Cricket's words shattered my hopes. "It never should have happened in the first place. You seem like a really nice guy. *So* nice. But I have my life in Vegas, and you don't even live in the state. We haven't so much as kissed and we're married? It doesn't make sense, and we have to put an end to it."

"It doesn't make sense." I saw my opening, and I was going to charge through it. "Just like it didn't make sense I was the one you barreled into in the hallway. Did it make sense you happen to have a headache just as I was bored and wandering through the different floors of this place? It didn't make sense that we got along so well, that we made a believable couple for Petesy and his new wife. And it didn't make sense that both you and I stumbled across the wedding chapel and decided it was a good idea to get married. That's a whole lot of happenstance. Coincidences left and right that led us to this very spot. It's fate. I don't think we should ignore it."

She blinked, her hands flat on top of the table. Our chipper server appeared at our booth with glasses of water. "Are you two ready to order?"

I lifted a brow at Cricket.

"No."

Was she answering me or the server? "We need a few moments yet, please." I didn't take my gaze off Cricket. I was tempted to order for her, but she was already spooked. There was no reason why I should know what she'd like to eat. It hadn't been on our short list of topics we discussed last night. But if I were to guess, I'd order her the strawberry cream cheese stuffed French toast. She wouldn't want to order it. Deep down, she'd tell herself she should get something like oatmeal and fresh fruit, but she was eating out, and special occasions demanded special orders, even if the event was an unplanned wedding.

"Maverick, listen to yourself. Vegas isn't fate. The city is known for people coming to town and doing things they never thought they'd do. They made it a marketing campaign." She waved her hands in the air and looked around. "We aren't special. How many couples do you think tied the knot when we did? At three in the morning?"

"I don't care about anyone else. I care about you. Us. All I'm asking for is three days."

"Why?" Her voice was near a screech. Disbelief radiated over her features like a beacon.

How did I convince her of nothing more than a gut feeling? If I couldn't get her to give me three days, how was she ever going to believe the real truth? How was she going to give up her job and her home to move halfway across the country? And then learn there were entire populations of people who were not human and could shift into creatures like wolves, bears, mountain lions, and most unbelievable of all, dragons?

"I saw you, and I wanted you." The truth my parents had preached was sometimes all we had. We could have the largest hoard of jewels known to dragon shifter kind. We could be from a ruling family. Everyone might even like us. But it would mean nothing if Cricket thought I was lying to her.

The truth is unwavering no matter what creature you are. Teenage me had rolled my eyes every time I heard that phrase. Adult me was hanging on to it with dear life.

"Why me?" She slumped, her expression lost and her eyes misting over. Was she going to cry? "Look at you. Guys like you go for women like Carrie."

When I opened my mouth, she waved me quiet.

"I'm not dissing myself. I happen to think I look just fine. I like myself. Respect myself. But the fact of the matter is we're all human. Hot men like you go after stunning women like my boss. She was why Peterson dropped me so fast. A hint of interest and he trashed a five-year relationship. That's reality. You and I are a mismatched package. So, why me?"

My future hinged on my answer. Telling her the truth had bought me time to explain, but she hit on the weak spot in the truth. *We're all human.* I wielded the truth again like a double-edged sword in the knife battle. "You are more beautiful than Carrie could ever hope to be. The goodness inside of you shines from the inside out, but I'm not only saying it's who you are that makes you breathtaking. It's your silky hair the color of brown topaz with the sun shining on it. The amber of your eyes with the darker flecks of rich brown are mesmerizing. The texture of your skin taunts me, no matter how far away I am. My fingers itch to touch you, to caress you, to have a chance to possess real treasure, if only for a few moments."

Her stunned stare stayed on me. Her lips were parted, but she didn't look ready to speak.

So I kept talking. "A lot of guys would think Carrie is beautiful, but she's not what calls to me. I could walk by a million women who are pure goodness inside and breathtakingly gorgeous outside, but the fact is, they're not you. You opened up to me after we bumped into each other. You trusted me to help you feel better. And then you gave me a chance by taking me to the reception. Our attraction? It isn't a one-way street. Guys like me know what we want, and I want you."

Her eyes were wide. "I don't know what to think," she said breathlessly. How could I get her to realize how she affected me?

"I get you're afraid to believe me. Assholes like Peterson have hurt you in the past. People like Carrie have made snide comments toward you your entire life. Humans are a complicated species. If I was a dog and my tail was wagging, my tongue hanging out, and I was nuzzling your hand, you'd have no trouble believing I like you." I never regretted being a dragon shifter, but I wished I could turn into a wolf to prove my point. A tail wagging on a dragon doesn't have the same symbolism.

"You're anything but a dog," she muttered. She scrutinized her menu, the adorable furrow back in her brow. Thoughts warred in her expression.

Doubt crept in. Why was I doing this? She didn't want to be with me, and long ago, I had vowed never again. Never again would I chase after a female and beg for her attention. Never again would I waste my time with someone who acted like I wasn't special to them. Astra had messed me up inside out and sideways, and I'd continued going back for more as if rejection had been a drug I was hopelessly addicted to. After all that, had I not changed?

But Cricket squared her shoulders, lifted her chin, and looked me directly in the eye. "Okay, fine. We'll try this for three days, but I'll have to tell my brother about us. He raised me since I was eleven, and he's probably not going to like you at all. You'll have Peterson to thank for that."

"I happen to be good at winning people over."

CHAPTER
THREE

averick

I SHOULD HAVE HEEDED Cricket's warning about her brother better. When she pulled up to the small corner condo she rented, a tall man with hair a few shades lighter than hers paced up and down her sidewalk.

We'd had a pleasant breakfast, getting to know each other. Cricket's brother was more like a father figure than a sibling. When their parents had died when she was in middle school, Vaughn was eighteen, and he'd raised her while finishing college and medical school.

At some point last night, she had messaged him, mostly gibberish. He'd been worried, rightfully so, and when she finally checked her phone, she nearly sprinted out of the restaurant. I'd reminded her of our deal—together for three days—and we'd driven to her place.

I was behind the wheel of her Accord. On the drive

here, she'd been on the phone with him, explaining the situation and urging her brother not to do anything stupid. What exactly that encompassed, I didn't know, and I didn't want to find out. I knew how close siblings were, and Cricket would pick him over me in a heartbeat. Three days wasn't a lot of time, and fighting with her brother would make my progress go backward.

Part of my job in Peridot Falls was to appease others. I was the buffer between the demanding people of the town and my sometimes crusty twin sister.

I got out of the car and was enveloped in the sweltering heat. Instantly, I missed the more humid summers at home. Still hot but not as bad as the desert and buffered by thick grass and billowy trees. There was so much stone in Vegas. Dirt and rock and concrete. No wonder my kind favored heavily wooded locations.

But those were my preferences. These surroundings were what Cricket had grown up in. Would she be willing to move? Would she be happy?

There was self-doubt again. What did I know about making a mate happy? I did nothing but fail for fifteen years. I was determined to be different. Nothing was the same about me and Cricket.

Before I could get to the other side of the car, Cricket jumped out and rushed to her perturbed brother. "Vaughn, I am so sorry—"

"Bug, what the hell?" He threw his hands in the air. "I've been frantic for hours. You shoot me photos of you and some guy I've never met before with words like 'congrats' and 'this is it' and 'fuck Petesy' and then go radio silent until after lunch?" His enraged gaze landed on me.

Cricket's brother was an inch or two taller than me but not as built. He had a muscular but lanky build, more like my brother. His wavy hair was brushed off his face, and the dusty-gray slacks and shimmery-pink collared shirt screamed corporate, but Cricket had said he was a physician. The arrogance plastered across his face fit either profession.

"I'm sorry, I'm sorry." She shoved her hands through her hair. "I wasn't acting like myself last night and things just happened, and I drank too much and—"

"And this asshole took advantage of you."

I stood my ground, hoping the altercation wouldn't get physical. Vaughn might know how to fight, he might even be stronger than me, but I guaranteed I had more experience than him. Dragon shifters were taught to fight, and not only in their dragon form.

Annoyance crossed her face. "No. He said I was too inebriated and didn't touch me."

Her brother only deflated slightly. "At least there's that." He jerked his dark hazel gaze to mine. "What the hell were you thinking, marrying her?"

I didn't have to plan my answer or come up with something believable on the spot. I gave him an abridged version of what I told Cricket. "I thought she was a treasure who was almost lost to a loser like Peterson. I've been through my own on-again, off-again toxic relationship, and honestly, I didn't know any better at the time. Now I do, and when I met someone like Cricket, it was easy to see what a diamond she is."

Vaughn stared at me for a heartbeat. His eyes narrowed like he was inspecting me for a glimmer of falsity. Cricket's gaze softened.

She studied the sidewalk until her brother replied. "While I'm relieved the only advantage you took of her was in the form of vows, we still don't know you."

Cricket shrank in on herself, swaying a little closer to me. I put my hand on the small of her back, a sign of encouragement, support that I was there with her. She wasn't facing her brother alone.

She didn't stiffen but was slow to meet her brother's gaze. "I've agreed to spend the next three days with him before we decide whether or not to end it."

Vaughn's eyes flared, disbelief slashing across his face like lightning. "You're getting an annulment immediately."

"We've made our decision," I said calmly.

This man radiated a sense of propriety around his sister. Protectiveness on steroids. While I respected their relationship, I couldn't have him overriding decisions Cricket and I had made together. She was an adult, intelligent, and we'd already had this discussion.

Vaughn's tone was sharp. "Are you saying she isn't free to change her mind?"

"Not at all," I replied, finding my calm, so I didn't escalate his emotions. "I'm saying I don't think you need to change her mind for her when she's already made it."

Cricket let out a choking cough. "I can't with this. I need some headache medicine and AC." She stormed toward the condo and banged through the front door. I was left with her brother on the sidewalk.

He glared at me. "I'm going to talk some sense into her."

I studied him. His jaw was set and unease radiated through his body like he wasn't used to being unable to intimidate someone. "I understand you two are close. But at some point, you need to let her make her own decisions and decide for herself what makes her happy."

"And you think you can make her happy?"

"I think I'll spend the rest of my life trying." I walked past him on the sidewalk. He didn't move, and our shoulders thumped together. "If you'll excuse me, I'd like to be with my wife."

~

CRICKET

THE MEETING with my brother could've gone better. He had called into the hospital to miss work and guilt gnawed at my stomach. Vaughn never phoned in sick. He could be closer to death's door than his patients, and he'd still show up with a pristine white lab coat, ready to crack a few jokes to ease the kids' anxiety. I hated taking him away from work.

I didn't want my brother and Maverick to fight. But in some ways, it would've been better. The icy tension chilled my living room to subarctic temps. It was like I was in the same room as two caged predators.

"What, exactly, do you plan to do hanging out for three days?" Vaughn paced the living room.

I sat on the couch with an ice pack at my forehead. Maverick had offered to do whatever magical thing he did last night to chase away my migraine, but I passed. The last time he put his hands on me, I said wedding vows. Who knew what the next time would bring?

"I don't care what we do." Maverick monitored me like he was waiting for my answer. "If you feel like sitting around and watching TV, that's what we'll do."

Vaughn snorted, making it sound like Maverick had no idea what my interests and hobbies were.

It was Saturday, and I'd planned to do just that. Veg in front of the TV and order delivery. I watched a lot of TV, and not that I thought it was a terrible habit, TV was my default. I had given my all to Peterson. We had done everything together, mostly because he hadn't created a relationship where outside friendships were encouraged. And I'd convinced myself he made me happy. All those connections were lost. My friends had moved on.

Would I like to snuggle on the couch and watch TV with Maverick? I'd be hoping to get naked the whole time. But Vaughn wasn't leaving and I couldn't take a day of this glacial tension.

"I'd like to go somewhere," I announced. The two men in the room waited for me to elaborate. I had nothing. "Maybe a water park? Red Rock Canyon?"

"There's a pool in my hotel," Maverick offered.

My brother scowled. "It's over a hundred degrees and you want to go hiking?"

It wasn't like me. It hadn't been like me. But what Vaughn didn't know was how often I had begged Peterson to leave the house, to go do something that wasn't sitting in a loud club having cocktails with his obnoxious friends.

"What's your favorite casino?" Maverick asked, his gaze intense like he was hanging on my answer.

"I haven't been to see the botanical gardens at the Bellagio. Everyone talks about how cool they are."

Vaughn propped his hands on his hips. "You should be getting this farce annulled."

Maverick's jaw hardened, but he kept his gaze on me. My stomach lurched. My mind and body didn't like the idea of letting Maverick go.

"It's in public." The best excuse I could come up with.

Excitement was starting to build. I had spent so many weekends at home when I wanted to be out exploring the world. I wasn't asking for a quick trip to Paris, just to go for a walk once in a while. "I have to shower first. You two try to behave."

I left them in my living room and went to the bedroom. After shutting and locking the door, I sagged against the wood and let out a deep sigh.

My overprotective brother was worried, rightfully so. But his attitude was getting more than a little embarrassing. Maverick had already seen me fighting a migraine because I was playing nice at my ex's wedding. Then he calmly explained to me the decisions I had made the previous night because I'd drunk too much to remember clearly. And now Maverick got to witness me being coddled, treated like I didn't know my own mind.

He was probably searching "How to annul a quickie Vegas wedding" while waiting for me.

But... on the off chance he wasn't repelled by me, I yanked my dress off and finished stripping down. It was tempting to stand under the shower's spray the rest of the day and forget what was outside the door. But despite what my brother thought, I wasn't one to shy away from the hard stuff. I used to like to tackle challenges. My years with Peterson had made me complacent. He was cautious, afraid of what others would think or that he'd look like less than the corporate business guy he strove to be. I'd grown up with Vaughn's support. Tackling college classes in high school, studying abroad during the summers, and then applying for jobs I thought were out of my league.

Peterson was the one who said I should apply for the accounts manager position. He claimed stability, but I think he was afraid to move. His father helped him get into a good college and his mother helped him get his fancy job. If we moved, he'd be on his own.

What was the saying? Don't let your significant other stop you from meeting the love of your life?

Had my ex helped me meet mine? Cold betrayal turned hot devotion?

I wanted to find out.

Shutting the water off, I twirled the gold band around my finger. It wasn't a two-carat flashy diamond like what Carrie wore. I remembered standing over a small case in the wedding chapel with sparkling diamonds blinking back at me. My attention kept drifting toward the gold band, and I'd made some comment about knowing I shouldn't pick something so simple. Maverick's reply still rang in my head. *Simple choices are sometimes the best ones. If it's what you want, fuck what anyone else thinks. But if you want jewels later, I have plenty you can choose from.*

You have jewels? I'd asked.

He nodded, no sign of a joke on his face. *I can't wait to show you.*

Are you, like, some kind of gem broker?

Collector.

Didn't Maverick say he worked in the city offices of his small town? How did a guy like that collect jewels?

Hopefully, I will get those answers and more in the next three days. And hopefully the answers wouldn't be the death of me.

FOUR

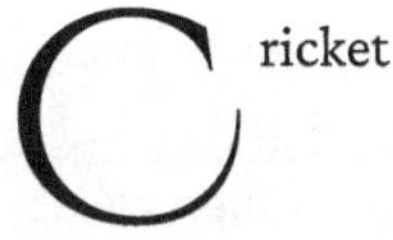

ricket

MY BROTHER TAGGED ALONG. How humiliating, but Maverick was a good sport. I stood next to a giant blue orb of flowers. My brother was standing several feet away, his nose tucked into his phone. He should have just gone back to work. I understood his caution, but I didn't have the same concerns as he did around Maverick.

Should I? Yes, but the only doubts and fears I could summon were that it wouldn't work out. His vibe was chill. Accepting. I craved it after being raised by my uptight brother, dating a pretentious jerk, and working for a superficial boss.

I was a city girl, but I'd grown up protected from a lot of the ugliness of the world. Still, I'd like to think I didn't lose my common sense when presented with a handsome man. An extremely good-looking face, with a sharp jawline, firm lips, a proud nose just shy of being too large for his face, but it only made him more attractive. And those startling eyes. Why did I have a feeling he saw more of the world with those eyes than I ever could?

"Are you hungry?" Maverick asked. "There are plenty of restaurants we can grab a bite."

A simple question but a stark contrast from Peterson. I hadn't noticed the barbed comments and the critiques of the food I ate, how much and what kind, until I was single and could eat judgment-free.

"I'm still full from the late breakfast." Our meal should've been lunch, but I didn't want to think about how late I had slept—or why. I wanted to get to know Maverick, not dwell on our vows.

"I imagine your brother will be joining us when we do have dinner?" A smile played over his lips.

"You're very accepting of his presence."

Maverick's sharp gaze strayed to where my brother paced by a brilliant mushroom of pink flowers with his phone to his ear. "I know what it's like to be a protective brother, even if Memphis can take care of herself."

"You mentioned you had a twin. What's that like?"

"I know no different. You could probably ask my brother Levi what it's like to have twins for siblings." He chuckled, deep and vibrating. I wanted to plaster my cheek to his chest when he chuckled to see how satisfying it felt.

"Instead of you being the middle child, he ended up being the stereotypical middle child as the youngest?"

"You could say that. He's recently opened my eyes to how badly he's been overlooked." Maverick rolled a big shoulder. "He's almost thirty, but it was hard not to see him as thirteen instead. It's been Memphis and I running the town since our parents passed away."

"What do you mean?" He made it sound like the Mafia, but I doubted there was a big mob problem in rural Minnesota.

His smile had a side of mystery. "She's the mayor, and I work for the city. But in a town that small, we each have a lot of departments under us."

"And what does your brother do?" I enjoyed learning about Maverick. I was glad we had the chance to take away the alcohol and see if this chemistry between us was real. A chance for me to see if this guy was legit.

"He's something of an entrepreneur." A large tour group was heading our way. He put his hand on the small of my back and gently led me down the meandering path. My brother shot him a dirty look but couldn't break away from his phone call. He ended up trailing behind us.

"He and his new mate—wife—recently opened a coffee shop and bakery. They're gathering data to see if the community can support rental cabins next."

"Fun."

The way he talked about his brother's wife was odd. "Why do you keep saying mate?"

Alarm flashed in his eyes, and the irritation I witnessed seemed directed at himself. "We have something of a different lifestyle in Peridot Falls. You'll learn that quickly enough if I can sweet-talk you into coming home with me." His look was playful, but his tone was serious.

I'd thought of leaving Vegas, but I got stuck when it came to leaving my brother. Vegas was large and bustling and hot and full of tourists most of the year. I had my tidy little condo, and I went to work. There was much more beyond those two destinations, but Vaughn was my only family. He was my best friend as much as my brother and leaving Vegas meant putting miles between us when distance had been temporary before.

I was thinking too much of myself in this situation. Maverick had committed early and hard. Why?

When we were far enough away from the large group behind us, I stopped. "I can't believe you're serious about this marriage thing."

"I know a good thing when I see it."

I sensed no guile, but I wasn't sure I could trust myself with being objective. If I could have a smidgen of the confidence Maverick had, I wouldn't have been at the wedding in the first place.

Vaughn got off the phone and shoved it into his pocket. "What'd I miss?"

Maverick shrugged, his easy acceptance of my brother's presence even more at odds with a guy who claimed to want me to himself. "I was trying to talk Cricket into coming to Peridot Falls with me."

Nothing like ripping the Band-Aid off. Vaughn's scowl deepened into a frown. "Why would she do that?"

"I'd like her to meet my sister and my brother. See the town. If I can't enchant her to move there, perhaps they can."

My brother's gaze slashed toward me. "You're not actually thinking of going?"

I wasn't sure, but his incredulous tone put me on edge. "I don't know, maybe. We are married after all."

For a girl who was just thinking how close to her brother she was, I was quick to antagonize him. But perhaps it was time to finally admit that his protectiveness had chafed all those years. His looming shadow was fine when I was surrounded by selfish friends with bad ideas. And his coddling had been needed after my breakup with Peterson. But this thing between Maverick and I, this marriage, wasn't something a brother could get involved in.

"Cricket, you can't be serious." Vaughn's exasperation grated on my nerves.

Maverick's hand was a steady presence on my back. He was close enough to feel the rise and fall of his chest at my shoulder. I barely knew him, yet I was seeking comfort in him.

"I don't know. I have three days to figure it out."

MAVERICK

I HAD Cricket to myself at her condo only because Vaughn could no longer be kept away from work. Throughout the day, there'd been an hour in total when he'd been off the phone. I hadn't minded; his distraction gave me a chance to get closer to Cricket.

Vaughn hadn't wanted to leave tonight either, but there'd been an emergency with one of his patients. I hoped everything was fine with the kid who was sick, but I might also send him a large bouquet of candy and toys for getting Cricket's brother out of my hair.

Cricket bustled around the kitchen, claiming to look for something to make for both of us for dinner. More likely, it was an excuse to distance herself from me now that we were once again alone under the same roof.

There'd be none of that. I had too much riding on our

nuptials. While I wasn't nearing my thirty-fifth birthday, I couldn't escape the urgency driving me to keep our vows intact. A human wedding meant nothing in my world, but the words Cricket and I had said last night to each other were everything. I needed to irrevocably tie her to me so when she found out what I really was, it wouldn't make a difference.

I prowled into the kitchen, the predator inside of me tracking its delicious, curvy prey. Her back was to me, and she was holding cupboard doors open, muttering to herself.

"Shells, rotini, spaghetti, no fucking sauce. I look like I eat worse than a college kid on a five-dollar weekly budget."

She didn't notice me. When I lightly laid my hands on her hips, she jumped, releasing the cupboard doors with a jerk. A yelp left her.

I nuzzled into her hair at the base of her neck. Her hair tickled my nose, wild and unkempt after her shower. I liked it. Her hair was like her—allowed to show its personality when it wasn't contained. "You don't have to stress about feeding me."

Resting her hands on the top of the island, she stiffened. "I didn't want to eat out again, but I usually buy groceries on the weekend and I thought the botanical gardens would be more exciting than the store."

I wouldn't have cared. Since I was likely the cause of her tension and not her dismal food choices, I pressed little kisses along her soft skin, releasing her hips only to move her hair out of the way. "There's only one thing in this kitchen I want on my tongue."

She jerked like electricity was running through my fingertips. "Maverick—"

"Shh." I slid one hand up her torso to cup a breast. A low groan rumbled out of me. She was soft, padded in all the right places, and ripe for my picking. I brushed my other hand over her belly and slipped beneath the waistband of her shorts and underwear. "Relax. I'll take care of you."

A portion of her tension drained out of her body. Her trust in me was humbling. I'd done little to earn it, and she was right to be wary, but not for the reasons most would assume.

I slipped my hand closer to heaven, her body growing hotter as I went. When I dipped over the curve of her mound, I was greeted with wetness. Another approving growl left my chest.

"Are you wet for me, Chirp?"

Of all the things I was doing, it was the nickname that made her melt into me. She didn't answer but let out a little mewl.

My new wife and the woman I hoped would be my mate needed this. Nothing propelled me more than the thought she craved a release, that she was okay with this. I would make sure she knew who was making her come.

I held her, one hand on her breast and my other down her shorts, with her hugged against my front. She'd feel my demanding erection prodding her lower back, but that could wait. I needed her to fall apart in my arms more than I needed my next breath.

I slipped my fingers through her wet seam until I hit her swollen little nub. It was tiny, plump, and perfect, just like her. She shifted her stance, widening her legs, giving me easier access.

"That's it, Chirp. I want to feel how hard you come for me."

"Maverick," she whined.

"Keep saying my name." I thrummed her clit. Her legs quivered and the counter was probably all that was holding her up. "Tell me you're mine."

Her eyelids fluttered as a wave of pleasure washed over her. She was close and so fucking wet it was all I could do not to drop to my knees and devour her until I hit her creamy center and she exploded on my tongue.

I sensed that was too much for her. But I needed something. I put my lips to her ear and growled, "You're mine."

"I'm yours?" she panted, straining for that elusive peak I was withholding from her.

I didn't like how she said it as a question. "Mine." I slid a finger into her, and goddamn, she was tight.

"Yours," she breathed.

"Good girl." I thrust in and out while I circled her soaking bud.

A low moan left her and she slapped the counter. "Oh god…"

She rode my hand, and I watched her come apart. This little human was at my mercy. She didn't play games with me. We were legally married, but she was honest about being unsure. Yet she hadn't shouted at me or run out of her house. She hadn't told me I was hard to figure out and not worth her time and to call her when I could grow the fuck up—

I wrenched my hand out of her shorts. Her eyes flew open and worry creased her brow as she looked over her shoulder.

Shit. I spun her around and kissed her on the mouth, not delving further. Then I kissed her forehead. "Sorry, I got in my head."

She stared up at me. The flush was leaving her cheeks much sooner than I wanted. "No, it's okay, I didn't mean to..." She glanced around the kitchen like this was all her fault.

I messed up, and I needed to explain, to tell her about me since that was the point of our time together. I just wished I wouldn't be so pathetic as I did it. "I wanted you. And, Cricket, there's nothing I want more than to be inside you right now and learn everything that you like. But it's too soon." I brushed the backs of my fingers from the hand that hadn't been getting her off down her cheeks. "I was thinking how different you are and it took me too far into the past."

"What do you mean?" Her question was cautious, guarded. We both had our shitty experiences with people who were supposed to lift us up instead of tearing us down.

I should move us to the couch to talk intimately, but I didn't want to break the spell, and we still needed to eat. "My ex, we used to... there were times... she was..." Sighing, I rested my hand on the counter behind her. This shouldn't be hard, but I didn't expect to be talking to my wife about my ex. "We'd been together since we were teens. I thought she was my mate, my forever, but we fought. She was supercritical, and for a long time, I was immature and I tried to piss her off. I used to love getting her riled up." I hung my head. I should've been better.

"Why?"

Why'd I start fights on purpose? It'd taken many years and a lot of lonely nights to figure it out. "I thought I deserved the screaming. Everyone thought we should be together. Her grandmother is on our city council, and she gushed about us. But I didn't... I went through the motions because I wasn't feeling it inside."

Understanding filled her eyes. "Oh, Maverick."

I shook my head. "No, I'm not the victim. We were young, and we both were horrible to each other, but even through that, I thought she was who I'd end up with. Then during our last breakup, she up and mated another guy almost immediately after. I was relieved, but also, damn."

Her forehead crinkled, and I knew it was because I said mate and mated, but I wanted to ease her into the differences between her and me. "She's married?"

"And still living in Peridot Falls, fair warning. But know that she's in my past."

Her expression was doubtful. "That's more than going to an ex's reception."

Did that mean she'd actually been considering going to Peridot Falls with me? "I fell out of love with her a long time ago. And it wasn't until now that I realized how differently I feel with you."

"Was she..." She chewed her lower lip. "You've been with more women than her?"

"During our off times, yes." Since Astra had been blatant with who she'd been fucking. Otherwise, I probably would've waited around like a lovesick sap in those early years. "I like being with you, Chirp. I feel good when I'm with you." I trailed my finger down her chest, wishing I'd taken her shirt off. "And I really fucking like it when you orgasm in my arms."

Her lips parted and a small huff came out. "You're a lot."

Grinning, I caged my arms around her. We needed to eat, but a little make-out session shouldn't be too much.

Her eyes lit like she would like the same. Freckles dotted her nose, and I was dying to know where else she had them on her body.

The front door banged open, and her brother called, "Sorry, Cricket. I didn't mean to be gone so long."

She closed her eyes. "He has a key."

And he wasn't afraid to use it. I stepped away from her, and as much as I hated washing her scent off me, I cleaned my hands at the sink. My intuition said she'd feel better if her brother didn't think I'd gotten her off in the kitchen while he wasn't hovering over her.

"Cricket!" Vaughn called.

"In the kitchen!" she hollered.

I dried my hands. "I'll find something to make. Go let your brother know you're safe."

"Thank you." Before she left, she stopped, putting her hand on my shoulder and her fresh linen scent surrounded me. "And thanks for sharing your past with me."

I didn't think I was making a mistake with her, but now I was convinced I didn't come to Vegas on a whim. Without thoughts of me and Astra, I could feel the person out there meant for me. In the end, it wouldn't matter if Cricket couldn't accept me for who, and what, I really am.

CHAPTER
FIVE

ricket

WHILE I HAD CALMED my brother's unreasonable panic, Maverick had stayed in the kitchen and found enough items to throw together for a meal. Pasta with homemade alfredo sauce. He could cook too.

Did I really need more convincing?

Yes. I was being responsible!

But that orgasm.... No. I couldn't just leave without thinking everything through.

My brother was important to me, he'd done so much, sacrificed a lot of his own life for me. But after what happened in the kitchen with Maverick, Vaughn's presence annoyed me. Not only was my body humming from the climax Maverick had so easily given me, but he had opened up to me. I'd learned more about him, and I wanted more details. More stories. More insight into the man who had been strolling around a Vegas casino all by himself.

I'd told Vaughn empty words when he'd returned. Stuff like "it'll all be fine" and "Maverick's been nothing but a gentleman." Words that were, for the most part, true, but I didn't think I'd ever be fine after having his hands all over me. He'd only used a few fingers to get me off, and the peak had hit harder and more powerful than any I had experienced with Peterson. My ex was watered down, and Maverick was pure moonshine.

"You can come and stay with me," Vaughn murmured. We were sitting in the living room. Maverick insisted on doing the dishes. My brother's brows were drawn together and he pressed the tips of his fingers together like he was conducting a board meeting. "Go pack a bag and we'll leave as soon as you're ready."

Jerked into the present, I blinked. The "no" that came out of my mouth surprised me and him.

"You can't possibly think it's a good idea to let him stay in your home," he hissed.

I needed to tread carefully. He was worried about me, but I wasn't. I fretted over my heart more than anything. Peterson's betrayal had destroyed me, and then Maverick had come along, treating me with kindness and respect I had rarely received from my ex. Peterson hadn't been abusive, but he'd been dismissive, of me, of my interests, of what was important to me. Peterson's world centered on him.

When Maverick's attention was on me, I felt like the only thing important in the universe. And for some reason, my gut told me that the man in my kitchen knew everything going on in the living room. He was attuned to me in a way I had never experienced and that I couldn't prove. Just a feeling, which had led me astray plenty of times before. But Maverick was different.

"Bug, you've gotta realize what a wild, impulsive, bad decision marrying him was." Vaughn lowered his voice to a ragged whisper, his worry punctuating every word. "You don't know him."

"That's why we're working on getting to know each other before we go through with the annulment." I had to get across to him how important this was to me, and when I couldn't fully explain it myself, the task grew more difficult. "We're pretending like the wedding never happened. Three days of dating. You wouldn't question if I dated a guy for three days, right?"

He gave me a flat look, and I sighed. Of course he would. He took his role as overprotective brother as seriously as his job in pediatric medicine. Only I wasn't a sick kid. I was a grown woman with my own mind and zero history of acting impulsively. Maybe I should've tried it a time or two, then I wouldn't have wasted so many years on Peterson.

"I'm taking three days and that's that." I leveled my most serious look on him. Between my tone and the finality of my statement, something should get through to him.

The muscles in the corners of his jaw flexed. "You're not letting him stay here tonight, are you?"

I didn't get that far in any of my planning with Maverick today. He made me want to run away from the fear this was all a dream, but I also didn't want to leave his side for the short time we had together. "I have plenty of room for him to stay here, if you're worried about something salacious happening."

His expression hardened. "I'm worried about the worst happening, Bug."

I let out a heavy sigh, understanding how daunting my brother's sense of responsibility could be. "You've already raised me, Vaughn. Now you have to trust me to make my own decisions—and my own mistakes."

He stared at me for a moment, his hazel eyes growing bleaker by the second. "I do trust you, but I can't risk losing you. It'll kill me to walk away and find out something happened that I could've prevented."

I put my hand on his shoulder and squeezed. "I know. But he's already had an opportunity to do horrible things to me and he didn't." And after getting a taste of what he could do to me, I regretted drinking too much and missing the chance. "I love you, but you're going to have to butt out of this one."

He tore his gaze away and stared at the woven rug in front of my couch. "Okay," he said hoarsely. "I'll give you space. But I'll be checking in."

"And I'll be answering." I patted his shoulder, filling my voice with authority to put him at ease. "Every time. You have my permission to charge to the rescue if you think something's wrong."

Maverick appeared in the entry between the kitchen and living room. He leaned his shoulder against the wall and shoved his hands into the front pockets of his jeans. "Dishes are done. We hanging here or going out? I'm good either way."

His timing was perfect. Between the relief of getting my brother to agree to back off and the casual way Maverick asked about what we were doing, I started laughing and couldn't stop. Maverick grinned, his eyes warming, and his wide smile highlighted the laugh lines in his features, making him impossibly more handsome. Vaughn glowered at the rug, no doubt hating the way Maverick and I acted like we shared an inside joke.

I seized the moment to answer Maverick's question and get my brother on his way. "Feel like a movie? Vaughn said he was taking off."

Vaughn rolled his eyes toward me. He knew what I was doing. "Fine. I'll go, but keep your phone on you."

"Of course."

He got up but hovered by the door. I rose to go to him, to reassure him I would be fine and he could go, but Maverick beat me to it.

"My sister's the same age as me, and she can kick my ass," he said. His body language wasn't dominant, but he faced my brother with a straight back and determined gaze. "I don't know what it's like to have a little sister or to have had to raise her, so I can't imagine what you're going through. I *swear* I won't hurt her."

Anybody could say the same words and not mean them, but there was a heaviness in the air once Maverick finished speaking. There was more significance in his claim, and I couldn't pinpoint why.

My brother must've felt the same charge. His expression flickered, and some of the doubt evaporated. "I'm going to check in."

"I'll make sure she hears her phone," Maverick replied.

I gave Vaughn a quick hug. He was tense, resistant to leaving, but he returned my embrace and then straightened. "Okay, well, good night then."

Once he left and the door was locked, I stood for a minute in case he came rushing back. I wouldn't put it past him, but at the same time, Maverick's vow must've been enough.

"Well, we're alone. Now what?" Too late, I realized how that could be taken. Innuendo where I had meant to make a joke.

"You're nervous." He wasn't asking.

I nodded, relief flowing through me thanks to his casual statement. He didn't seem perturbed about the walls I was erecting between us now that it was just him and me. "What we did earlier was... really nice." Understatement of the year. "But I really do feel like we should get to know each other better first."

"No problem. Do you like to watch movies?"

"I watch way too many movies." If putting on a sappy show that left me bawling and running through a box of Kleenex for the last few months was a hobby, then yeah, I liked to watch movies. "Do you? You don't look like a guy who sits in front of the screen long."

The corner of his mouth hitched up. "I have a fast metabolism. It runs in the family."

"Lucky."

He closed the distance between us before my brain registered he had moved. His hands were at my hips, and he was speaking low before I could grow alarmed. "Your curves are magnificent, and while I only want you to be happy and feel comfortable in your own skin, don't think for one second you'll ever need to change yourself for me."

Tentatively, I licked my lips, trying to get some moisture back into my suddenly dry mouth. His gaze tracked my tongue, and I had a hard time concentrating on what I meant to say. "I... I guess it's just ingrained in me to always want to be skinnier and prettier."

"I understand. Hazard of society, but just know that I don't fucking care. This ass?" He ran his hands over my hips to my butt cheeks. "Has been on my mind since the moment I first saw you."

"That wasn't even twenty-four hours ago."

"And it feels like an eternity because I don't get to be inside you. But don't take that as pressure. Just know it won't matter. Five hours or fifty years, I'm going to want to tap that."

Fifty years? I choked on my response. "Are you for real? It's like the universe plucked a fantasy I didn't know I had right out of my head, and poof—you materialized. You can't be real."

"You'll learn soon enough there's more to me than I can tell you now. There's more to my family and where I live, and it'll seem fantastical, but fundamentally, it doesn't change who I am."

Confusion blurred my good mood. When a guy showed you his red flags, you should believe him. A sliver of warning tracked through my brain, but Maverick's proximity robbed me of caring. At the moment, he could tell me he was a serial killer with a fetish for smelling women's used underwear and I'd have a hard time justifying opening the front door and telling him to leave.

"You're dangerous." On so many levels.

"You have no idea." He brushed a finger down my cheek. "But not to you."

Was that red flag number two or just an extension of the first one? Maybe it was time to start asking some hard questions. I'd start with the odd things I'd noticed about him. "Why do you say mate?"

Amusement danced in his greenish-yellow eyes, but there was a thread of underlying concern buried so deep I almost missed it. "It's part of what sets my family apart from others."

Releasing my ass, he grabbed my hand and tugged me toward the couch. He sat in the corner and drew me toward him until I was on his lap, my back nestled into his chest.

As much as I liked this position, I couldn't let it cloud my thinking. "That didn't answer my question."

"My truth is a bit of a paradox. There's a whole history behind my family that dictates my present, but it's a secret we can't tell outsiders until they're committed to us."

Was speaking in riddles a third red flag? He tightened his arms around me.

"I'm not telling you to coerce you into staying with me. I'm stating a fact. It's dangerous for you to know what I am, what my family is, who my people are without being committed to us—completely."

"Committed? Like sister wives?" A part of me was considering just how many other wives I'd be willing to share him with. Would I get a night like this once a week, twice a week? Could I keep my jealousy at bay and settle for scraps of attention? Ridiculous. I didn't do polygamy, and the thought of Maverick passing from woman to woman before he came to me inspired irrational anger.

His deep chuckle vibrated into my back. "No sister wives. You're my only wife, and if you stay with me, you'll be my only forever."

God, that sounded nice.

His chin rested on my head. "There are parts of this world the majority of the population doesn't know about. And even if they saw the proof right in front of their eyes, they wouldn't be able to explain it."

"Like psychics? Do you come from a family of witches?"

His breathing grew shallow. "Do you believe in witches?"

His question was cautious, like he wanted a truthful answer and not for me to laugh it off. "I didn't beyond all the fairy tales growing up. But I know witchcraft is making a comeback in modern society. Whether I believe there's any actual power behind their spells or whatever they do?" I lifted a shoulder and thought about it. "I guess I believe there's stuff out there I don't understand and that maybe it isn't for me to mess with, so I've never been interested in exploring."

"It's for the best. A lot of people don't know what they're really getting into." He nuzzled my hair. For such a big man, he was quite cuddly. "And no, my family aren't witches."

"Warlocks?"

More laughter resonated between us. "Not warlocks either. Soon, I'll be able to show you."

Soon, but not here. "Not in Vegas?"

"Not in Vegas," he confirmed.

I rested my head on his shoulder, and he pressed a kiss into my hair. I was falling for him so hard, and we hadn't had sex yet. I wanted to, and I wanted more of this. Talking to him, learning about him, and my curiosity was growing insatiable. What was with his family that he couldn't tell me in the privacy of my home? How, exactly, was he dangerous?

He said he wasn't dangerous to me, but he was. He could walk out the door, never to be seen again, and I'd cry harder over him than Peterson. So, if I was this far gone, why not go all the way? Why not take the chance?

"I want to see your home."

His hold tightened briefly. "You do?"

"I feel like in the morning, I'll open my eyes and find out this was all a dream. Or that you'll toss me off the couch, laughing, and tell me it's a joke."

He was opening his mouth, so I charged ahead.

"But in case neither of those things is what's going on, I'd like to stay with you. I was born and raised in Vegas. I'll take the gamble."

"You're not gambling, and I'll make sure to prove it." He grabbed the remote and clicked the TV on. The hard ridge under my hip was undeniable. He'd been hard since the moment he pulled me on top of him, but he didn't thrust into me or discretely try to rub one off. He'd let me talk, and he held me like he cared. The difference from what I experienced in the past was stark.

I thought of what we'd done earlier and how amazing it felt. I wanted to do the same for him. In fact, watching a movie perched on top of his erection didn't sound nearly as fun as learning what was really going on behind the zipper of his jeans. But I relaxed into him, enjoying the proof of how I affected him and knowing going any further would be too much for me.

As we picked out a show, he cradled me in his lap, and I felt precious. That was enough for tonight.

CHAPTER

SIX

Maverick

WAKING up to my future mate would never get old. This morning, she wasn't mildly hungover and confused. She opened her eyes like she was shocked I was still there, that I didn't disappear when her dream dissipated.

"Morning." I kept my boxer briefs on last night when I crawled under the covers with her. She'd fallen asleep during the movie and I carried her to the bed. She had woken up when I laid her down but fell asleep as soon as I crawled in behind her and cradled her in my arms.

Surprisingly, I had gotten some rest too. Half my blood supply perpetually rerouted to my dick as soon as I laid eyes on Cricket and her lush body, another portion had allocated to my erection when I'd been rubbing her to a hard climax, and after a second night of having lain next to her, I was in pain unlike I'd ever known.

"Morning," she said in an adorably groggy voice. Her eyes widened, and she flipped over to grab her phone.

"He's only messaged once." Any more, and I would've woken her rather than face an angry brother barging through the front door.

Her fingers flew over the keypad and she muttered as she typed, "I'm here, I'm fine, I'm not ravaged."

"What every brother loves to hear."

She smiled and rolled back toward me, keeping to the edge of her side of the bed. "What are we going to do today?"

"The hotel has a spa. When's the last time you had a massage?" I'd love to be the one to do it, but I couldn't until she was comfortable going all the way. I would restrain myself as long as I needed to, and I could endure a lot of pain, but I wasn't a masochist.

Interest lit her eyes. "A massage?"

My decision was made. Cricket was getting pampered all day. Last night when we'd talked on the couch, I had grown more optimistic she would follow through and come to Peridot Falls with me. Perhaps a day of spoiling her would clinch the deal, take away the worries that would prevent her from giving in to us.

"I'll use the bathroom first," she said breathlessly as she rolled out of bed. She'd stayed in her clothes and I hadn't urged her to change. Barriers made her feel comfortable.

On my back, I stared at the ceiling and contemplated my next move. Thinking was pointless while my heartbeat and my concentration were zeroed in on my cock. I was a grown man; I could control myself. But damn, I was uncomfortable. I wanted more of her. How did she taste? Was she as sweet and creamy as she looked?

Before I knew it, I was waiting outside the bathroom door, tracing the grains of the wood with my eyes as if my pupils were lasers that could burn the door down. I wouldn't intrude on her while she showered. She needed to trust me. But I could be honest. If she stayed with me, this wouldn't be the first time she faced a horribly aroused Maverick Peridot.

The water kicked off and I could hear her humming. Just like I'd heard the entire conversation she had with her brother on the couch. Neither of them could know how seriously I took my vow of not harming her. Cricket would learn the repercussions of breaking a vow soon enough when she learned about my kind, but for now, it was enough that she sensed my promises weren't arbitrary.

The sounds of her moving around in the bathroom shouldn't be an erotic dance, but I was in bad shape. My erection tented the underwear so badly the band was pulling away from my body. I was growing light-headed like I couldn't get enough oxygen to my brain, and my mouth watered for just one little morsel of her.

I heard the sound of the light switch flick off right as the door opened. She jumped, her body wrapped in a plush robe. "Maverick." A tremor went through her that I hoped was a thrill, not fear.

"I want to get between those legs of yours and devour you. Please." My voice was ragged. "Let me taste you."

Her wide gaze dropped to my raging erection. I didn't look down, but I knew she'd see the head of my cock poking out of my underwear. Those pretty lips of hers parted, and I groaned. That startled gaze shot back up to my eyes. "You want to..."

Her blush was killing me. The scent of her arousal

curled around my nostrils and I was moments away from shredding my underwear off my body. I couldn't take one more ounce of discomfort. I wouldn't touch her if she didn't want me to, but goddamn, I was miserable. I'd drain every drop of cold water from Las Vegas if she turned me down.

"Yes," I said, heaping more honesty on her that might scare her away. "There's nothing I want more right now than to make you scream my name while you're coming."

Her inhale was more like a gasp, but her hands fell to the belt tied around her robe. "I'm afraid to say yes."

"I won't touch you until you do." I had never wanted anyone so badly. Not with my ex, not when we were broken up, and I was lonely, not ever.

When the whisper of the "yes" left her mouth, I briefly closed my eyes. "Thank fuck."

I backed her against the bathroom counter and dropped to my knees. The front of her robe fell open, and I drank her in, running my hands up her thighs, toward her round hips, and over the fullness of her belly. "You're so damn beautiful."

In one move, I propped her legs on my shoulders and claimed her clit. She bucked against my face, her hands gripping the edge of the counter, and my name flew from her lips. "Maverick. Oh my—" The rest was swallowed by a moan as I devoured her.

Her legs quivered next to my ears, but her peak was coming fast and hard. I couldn't take the time to put a finger inside of her, I was too desperate to taste her orgasm on my tongue.

I didn't realize I was growling right away, and when I did, I didn't bother to stop. I was part animal after all.

"Mav—" Her legs tightened around my head. I

wouldn't die, but I'd gladly suffocate and pass out, only to wake up with my tongue on her hot little bud. "Oh my god—Maverick!"

Her cries echoed through the bathroom. My name, exactly what I'd wanted. I drank her down and kept going.

She shoved a hand in my hair, down to its roots, as she writhed against my face. "Maverick, I don't think I can—"

I cut her off with another growl and thrust two fingers inside of her. The moan I wrung from her was pure heaven on my eardrums. I continued my assault until I earned another orgasm.

She was going boneless, and my ego was inflating bigger than Nevada, but her legs were losing strength. I could feel them sliding off my shoulders, and one of my hands was quite busy. I couldn't hold them both up for her, and I wanted so badly to put my cock where my fingers were.

I dragged my tongue through her folds one last time and carefully rose, going slowly so she could hook her feet behind my waist. I didn't move my hand but lazily thrust my fingers in and out of her while I did nothing but rest my thumb close to her dripping clit.

Limp legs were hooked around me, the rest of her was sprawled across the bathroom counter. The top of her shoulders rested against the mirror and the flush from her face went from her cheeks down to the tips of her rosy breasts.

"I could do this all day and never tire of it." I dipped my head and caught one of her taut pink nipples in my mouth. She wrapped both her hands in my hair and whimpered, but she didn't push me away.

While she arched into my mouth, I took my time finger fucking her and switching my attention from breast to breast. I needed this time to calm down. Standing, my erection was dangerously close to that hot, wet center of hers. Too close to where I could come inside her tight little body. Nothing but my hand was blocking the way, and that was an easy enough obstacle to move.

Determined to be a gentleman and prove myself worthy of her trust, I continued tonguing her nipples to keep myself from kissing my way up her neck and sinking a claiming bite into that tender flesh. Everyone would know she was mine. Marriage was a weak human custom compared to mating, and mating could be nothing but an agreement, a bond between two people that didn't have to mean more than two people were bonded. A claiming bite would mark her as mine. Any shifter she came across would know she was taken.

But until she understood the significance, my teeth had to stay far away from her neck.

She was squirming under me, a delicious sensation I was the root cause of. The roll of her hips matched the thrust of my fingers.

"Maverick?" Her voice was strained, breathy.

"Yeah?"

"I need more." Her gaze dropped to the broad head of my cock pushing past the waistband of my underwear.

"Do you want me to fuck you, Cricket?" There'd be no mistake what we were doing. No excuses for her to hide behind.

She nodded, the undulation of her hips getting stronger.

"I don't have protection on me. There'd be nothing between us." I didn't come to Vegas looking to get laid. I didn't even have a condom in my wallet, which lay on the floor of the bedroom. "But I swear you won't get a disease from me."

It didn't work that way between shifters and humans, but I couldn't exactly say it like that.

"I'm still on birth control."

I kept up the steady in and out of my fingers, giving her a chance to back out.

She didn't, and I had a decision to make. Do I fuck her on the bathroom counter or waste precious seconds getting onto the bed?

There was no reason I couldn't do both.

I tore my underwear off, ignoring the bite of the ripping seams against my skin. And then I was pushing inside of her, into the sweltering hot welcome of her tight body. She gripped my shoulders.

"Maverick." The sound was half pleasure, half anxiety.

"You can take it, Cricket. Trust me." From her reaction in the kitchen, I could tell she hadn't been fucked properly, but I hadn't known what equipment Peterson was working with until now. And maybe it wasn't the equipment, but the delivery. "Open those legs wider, baby."

She did as I asked, and I captured her mouth in a long, passionate kiss. Sliding my tongue along hers had the intended effect. She relaxed, and I pushed all the way in. The beast inside of me wanted to toss skill and control out the door and randomly thrust until I detonated inside her.

The beast was me, and I was in control. When she was warm and pliant in my arms, I rocked my hips. Pulling back, I wanted to watch myself stroke in and out.

Her eyelids fluttered open, and she pinned me with a flushed gaze.

I was gripping her hips so hard she'd probably have fingerprints embedded in her skin. But she wasn't complaining. She moved in the same rhythm as me. I deliberately dropped my gaze to where my soaked erection thrust in and out and the greedy way her body gripped me. When I glanced back up at her, she was watching the same thing.

"Look what you do to me. This is where I've wanted to be since I first saw you. No matter what, never doubt me." I didn't know what made me add the last part. I'd been so preoccupied with getting her to come home with me, I didn't think about what we'd do after. There was the huge obstacle in between—telling her I was a dragon shifter and teaching her about our world.

But there was more, and it didn't matter that I was ready to come, all the baggage from my past relationship piled into my brain. I couldn't lose Cricket due to jealousy or some other bullshit misunderstanding. People would talk. They would tell her things. But she was mine.

"Fucking mine," I ground out.

"Yours," she echoed.

My gaze flew to hers, but her head was lolling back against the glass. She'd said it without realizing what it meant, or what it did to me.

I was so damn close to coming, but I couldn't yet. We were hitting our peaks together, and I didn't care how many times I got her off. I tapped a thumb against her rosy pink clit, and she bowed into me, my name coming out on a moan.

"You're coming again." My thrusts were growing

more erratic, and I was slamming into her harder. "We're in this together."

"Together," she whined at the precipice.

I pumped into her once, twice more, and her body tightened, gripping my cock like a blistering fist. Fireworks exploded behind my eyes as I gritted her name out between my teeth and released inside of her.

This was how it was supposed to be.

I didn't track how long my aftershocks lasted. All I cared about was the trembling Cricket in my arms who could barely keep her legs anchored around my waist.

"I don't think I'm going to survive, Maverick," she murmured, her eyes droopy.

"I'll give you life." And I did. Just like when she'd had a headache, I infused her with some of my healing energy, weak as it was. It still did the trick.

She ran her hands behind my neck, her fingers fiddling with the ends of my hair. "Why do I feel like I just got a vitamin shot?"

I chuckled, sinking against the counter while still inside of her. "I'll explain that later too. But right now, I can tell you I have a lot more stamina than anyone you've ever been with."

She frowned like she didn't want to talk about past partners, and I didn't blame her. Neither did I, but those fuckers were going to get in the way of our future if we let them. Might as well be transparent about all the shit they put us through now.

"I've only been with one guy before." The self-consciousness in her voice almost did me in. Her experience, or lack thereof, didn't bother me. I gathered her into my arms, and without removing myself from her body, I carried us to the bedroom, shedding her robe as we went.

"Then allow me to help you forget him."

~

CRICKET

I NEVER KNEW sex could be like this. As cliché as it sounded, it was God's honest truth. Maverick and I had stayed in bed all day yesterday, having sex and talking about our families. For not getting out of bed, I was still exhausted enough to fall asleep in his arms. And this morning, I didn't shower alone. He had pushed in with me, and I had totally let him. I'd hoped he would.

I should be sore in places I didn't know existed, but somehow after every time we did it, I was flooded with soothing energy, just like when he'd chased my migraine away. But even without whatever magic his fingers and his penis possessed, I didn't feel used. We'd talked so much I felt like I knew him as much as I knew my brother. More, probably. Vaughn took care of me, but we didn't have a lot of heart-to-hearts. He was a closed-up man, and I liked to think he would find someone like I did and open himself up to happiness.

I was cautiously happy. Maverick had told me about Memphis and Levi. He told me all about when he'd first met Levi's mate—now I'd started using the term.

He talked about a neighboring town and its mayor. And he told me about a few other small towns in North Dakota he had visited recently. He claimed they were all "his people."

Today was his last day in Las Vegas. We had run to his motel room so he could pack his bags and check out.

We had sex there too. He'd grumbled about sleeping next to me that first night, not touching me, saying he wanted to know what it was like to have me in this bed. I'd never felt so wanted or cherished. As the time for him to leave town approached, I had a decision to make. Was I really leaving with him?

I pulled into my garage, and he parked his pickup in the driveway. I stared at my steering wheel, not moving, while my mind churned over possibilities. Did I stay, or did I go?

My door opened, and he propped himself in the gap, his strong arms stretched wide, showing off the natural taper to his waist.

"I don't want you to leave," I said honestly, my throat raw.

"I don't want to be apart from you." He stroked a finger down my jaw. "I've just found you."

He said the sweetest things. How could I not trail him back to Peridot Falls and find out where we would go?

"I'm going." There. My decision was made.

His brows lifted, and he stepped back, holding a hand out for me. I accepted his help getting out of my car. We stood in the dark garage facing each other. My body hummed from what we'd done earlier in the day. Another reminder of why I wanted to plaster myself to his back and never let go.

"Are you sure?" His brow was furrowed like he was worried I would regret my decision. His scrutiny was intense, as if he was willing me to backpedal just to make sure I was committed to my answer.

"Yeah. You fucked some sense into me."

A startled chuckle left him. "I want you to come with

me more than anything. But I also know it's your life that will change. Mine cannot."

He spoke as if I couldn't return to Vegas. As if we couldn't just divorce and go our separate ways. It had to do with his cryptic information about how different he and his family were. I refused to believe I was entering some sort of cult that would keep me prisoner. Besides, if I went off the grid, Vaughn would come searching for me.

Didn't mean I would tell him I was going until I left. I wouldn't put it past him to lock me in a closet while he drove Maverick away. Not that I thought he could outmuscle Maverick, but I didn't want to find out.

Inside, I dragged out two big suitcases and filled them with shoes and clothing. Maverick wandered through the kitchen and living room while I packed my toiletries. A lot more than he had in the hotel. Yet his hair was stylishly brushed to the side, looking like he could model for a business ad, while I was the before photo for a conditioner commercial.

"We can fit a lot in the back seat. Don't be afraid to pack more," he said as he breezed into the bedroom to haul my luggage out before I had the chance to lift them.

"I can always come back for more." I hoped I would be coming back for more and not returning for good. The last few days with Maverick were mind-blowing. I would more than miss it; I would be destroyed. "I'd have to sell the condo and get my car to Minnesota." There was one task I needed to do first. "I should call work."

The decision to move came with an epiphany. I wanted to quit my job. I didn't mind the mundane work I did, but working for Carrie the last few months was demoralizing. Demeaning. Breathing the same air as her while she either didn't notice or didn't care about what she'd done to me was torture. I might have Maverick, and he might have shown me how lacking my relationship with Peterson was, but that didn't mean I wanted to return to an environment of continual disrespect. I was over my ex. I was over what he and Carrie did to me. But I would not tolerate their presence any longer. If I found myself back in Vegas, I'd find a new job. And if my income became a worry, then I'd move in with Vaughn, and that'd be enough motivation to get my ass out looking for a job. I loved my brother, but I wasn't going to be his roommate.

"You want privacy for the call?" Maverick shut the back door of his pickup. "Do you need to stop and give your notice in person?"

The continuous respect I got from Maverick confirmed my resolve. Carrie had gushed about her big honeymoon at the end of the month. They couldn't coordinate a wedding and vacation on such short notice. Another reason why I had taken today off from work. I didn't need to waste one more second as her employee.

"No, I'll call when we're on the road."

After a final check through the condo, we drove away. I brought up Carrie's office number, mentally formulating the message I would leave.

She answered, and I nearly dropped the phone, startled. How quickly my determination faded.

No. I was going through with this. "Hey, Carrie. It's Cricket. I'm—"

"Cricket?" she whined. "I was just going to have Jill call you. I know it's your day off, but we really need you to come in and finish the Madison report. Mr. Becker wants it by the end of the month, but as we all know, I'll be on the beach in St. Martin's by then—"

"I quit." She was going to call me in on my day off? My day off, after she married my ex six months after we broke up?

Carrie gave a nervous, disbelieving laugh. "Cricket, be serious. We have a lot to get done before I go on my honeymoon."

I couldn't stand her singsong tone. She'd used it to snow me over one too many times.

"See, the thing is, I've never been so serious, Carrie. I met someone, and not only did it show me how utterly disrespectful you and Peterson are, but helped me understand that I don't have to tolerate you or your behavior anymore at work."

There was a beat of silence. "Where's this coming from? Peterson and I have been nothing but considerate of your feelings."

My laughter drowned out anything she would've said after that. "The only thing you can be considerate about is yourself. I quit. For now, you can send anything to my home address, otherwise I will be enjoying my own honeymoon with my new husband." I hung up.

Stunned, I stared out the window. Did that just happen? Had I told anyone off in my life? In the grand scheme of things, what I said to Carrie was mild at best. But for me, it was huge. I'd sat through months of listening to her gush about the man who'd broken up with me for her. I'd worked extra hours so she could take time off to plan the wedding, and she was going to call me in on my day off so I could get her responsibilities finished before the honeymoon.

"I can't believe I just did that," I murmured.

"She has some balls."

I lifted a brow. "Did you hear all that?" Carrie's voice was high-pitched, but she wasn't overly loud.

"I have good hearing."

I let my gaze drift over his strong profile as he kept his eyes on the road and his roped forearm draped over the wheel. "Another one of those family traits?"

He flicked his gaze toward me, and a knowing smile played over his lips.

I let out a small laugh. My phone started buzzing with calls and messages. Both Carrie and Peterson were blowing up my line. "I think she recruited Peterson to talk me into coming in to work." I shut my phone completely off and tossed it into my tote bag. "Or to tell me to fuck off, but I'm sure Carrie wants him to talk me into doing half her work before their honeymoon."

His gaze dropped to the tote bag and went back to the road. "Smart move, but won't your brother try to reach you?"

Oh crap. He would. What if Peterson tried to call him? A long sigh leaked out from between my lips. "I guess I should tell my brother sooner rather than later. I was hoping to make it to Peridot Falls."

"It's a solid two-day drive, three days if you want to stop and sightsee. Since I was supposed to leave today, he's going to check on you."

Reluctantly, I dug my phone back out and turned it on. Missed calls from both Peterson and Carrie. The barrage of messages was easy enough to block. I did the same with their numbers. It'd be fun to respond with some profanity-laced comebacks, but they've taken enough of my time.

I was about to type out a message to Vaughn when I thought better of it. Instead I called him. His phone went right to voice mail. I wasn't prepared to leave a message, but he deserved at least that.

"Hey, I know you're going to be upset because I didn't tell you in person, but I'm leaving today with Maverick. I'll keep you updated on my whereabouts and how it's going, but my decision has been made. I also quit my job, which I would've done if I had left Vegas or not. So in case you hear from Peterson, go ahead and tell him to fuck right off. Love you, and try not to worry so much."

I tossed the phone in my bag again and put my head on the headrest, letting all the air escape out of my body.

Maverick flipped on the radio. "What would you like to listen to?"

The corner of my mouth kicked up. It was time to learn about each other and our tastes. We might be compatible in bed, but were we good enough together to survive a twenty-hour trip?

"I love listening to true crime podcasts."

His laughter was deep, and he tossed me his phone. "Pick one out. I'll try anything once."

I didn't know what was in store for me once we reached our destination, but we were going to have a good time on the way there.

averick

My stomach was clenching into a tight knot the closer we got to Peridot Falls. Night had fallen. We'd made the trip in two days, and it was getting late. Cricket hadn't been interested in sightseeing, as nervous as me, but for other reasons. She was probably worried if my sister would like her. What would my brother think of her? Would she run into my ex? Minor concerns compared to mine.

I should've handled this differently. I should've done more than reply to Memphis's and Levi's messages that I was doing fine. I should've told them about Cricket.

But I didn't.

And now the time of keeping her under wraps, of being in our own little bubble that my shifter world couldn't reach, was coming to an end. Cricket would have to learn what I was. She'd have to learn about my people.

She'd have to commit herself to me and total secrecy, or she'd pay the high fine—with her life.

I thought of what shifter kinds' overall leader did. When his human mate first rejected him after promising to be his, he stood in her place to take the punishment. He was willing to trade his life for hers. I would do it for Cricket in a heartbeat, but the one tasked with killing me for telling a human who didn't commit themselves to the clan would be Memphis.

How could I do that to her?

So, yeah, I'd stayed in the bubble with my wife. I didn't want Memphis or Levi to worry for days before it was necessary. I trusted my siblings, but word had a way of spreading, and I didn't want people ready to share with Cricket the sordid details of my tumultuous past with Astra.

But it was time to push a pin into the bubble.

We were right outside of Peridot Falls. I was already going into town with a giant surprise. My sister would be hurt and upset. She'd feel betrayed, and I didn't know about Levi. He'd recently been on my ass for not treating him like an equal but an annoying little brother. This wouldn't help.

I wasn't that close to anyone else. I'd dated Astra. And when I was single, I fucked around. It'd been nothing but wasting time in an attempt to feel less alone. Nothing like it was with Cricket, but she might get the wrong impression when she was stuck in city limits with females who'd been with her husband.

Fuck, I wished I could leave Peridot Falls. But my duty was there, and... I wouldn't want to live anywhere else. This was home. These were my people. Nothing had bothered me before, but that was before I found a human I wanted so badly to be my mate.

"Hey, when we get to my sister's house..." I needed Cricket to understand why I'd been silent. As much as I could share with her before I showed her how I could turn into a dragon and belch fire.

She blinked at me, her eyes wide against the dash lights. They made her look younger, more innocent. Like I was bringing a virgin home to sacrifice.

I'd made damn sure she wasn't virginal. It was all I could do not to stop one more time and take her in the back seat like we'd done in the middle of nowhere in Wyoming.

Might as well rip the bandage off. "I haven't told my family about you yet."

Her recoil was slight, but the faint scent of hurt gutted me. "Oh."

"It's not why you think, and it has to do with what I'm going to show you once we're settled." I wiped a hand down my face. Shadowed trees crowded the road. We were miles away from the turn to Levi's place.

Memphis lived on the edge of town, but I planned to go to my place first and tell her to come over. The less the townsfolk saw of Cricket, the better. The less Cricket saw happening after dark, the better.

"You don't think she'll like me?" Insecurity poured out of her voice.

"It won't have anything to do with you. She's going to be hurt I didn't tell her, but she's going to be worried. If you don't... if you can't..." I blew out a hard breath. Dots of lights from houses were the only announcement we were in Peridot Falls. We didn't have a lot of streetlights, and we didn't need them. Shifters could see just fine in the dark. Peridot Falls didn't have many human mates. Levi's mountain lion shifter mate was one of the few other non–dragon shifter mates. People wouldn't have a problem with Cricket's humanity. They'd have a problem if she had a problem.

"A lot is riding on your acceptance of me. And them. And if you don't... it can get bad."

"For me?" she squeaked.

"I won't let anyone hurt you."

She drew back. "Implying they would want to?"

"We have a law—It's not something I can tell you without showing you. Tomorrow, okay?"

"Maverick—"

"Cricket, I promise." I'd already given my word to Vaughn. I wasn't making promises willy-nilly, but the gravity was in my voice. "Promises to our kind are different. We're serious when we make them."

Her gaze swept across the shadowed town. A half-moon hung over the sky, highlighting nearby clouds. As much as I wanted to kiss the fear away, we were entering what would likely be the hardest part of our relationship.

I hit the button for my garage and it opened.

"Your house looks nice," was all she said.

She couldn't see much other than an old two-story farmhouse. With all the trees, a taller house worked better than a wider house. The rooms were small and while her condo had been older with a more closed floor plan, it didn't compete with my place. But Peridot Falls didn't have a lot of new construction.

She got out and awkwardly waited while I hauled out her bags and mine. I only let her take one of hers since she'd feel better having something to do.

Inside, I flipped the light switch on, cringed, and waited for her reaction.

"It's…" She stopped with a frown.

"A work in progress." The cabinets were ripped out. I'd taken the blinds off the kitchen windows. I led her farther in. We'd have to walk through the entire first floor to get to my room—our room.

"Oh…"

Yeah. She'd noticed the half-painted walls, going from some bullshit purple to a standard new-build white. The rugs had been hauled out before I left, leaving bare hardwood that needed a polish. The walls were missing pictures. Just ones of me and my siblings and my parents when we were younger remained.

My bedroom wasn't any better. If anything, it was worse. The mattresses were new though.

Damn, how could I have forgotten what a state of disarray I'd left my place in? The blinds were also off the windows. "If you go into the bathroom, there's only the plain shower curtain liner. No mats. You'll have to put a towel on the floor."

She raised a brow. "Is this your normal?"

The hopeful tone in her voice prompted a smile. "No. Ah… Astra's mating was a surprise, and I wanted any trace of her gone from this place."

Her gaze swept my bedroom again, landing on the new mattress that needed sheets. Then she nodded. "I get that."

"I'm glad I did it now, but I wish I could've finished the renovations before you arrived." I shoved my bag toward the folding closet doors and crossed to her. I put my hands on her shoulders. "I'd rather have a blank slate to start with you."

The worry softened in her gaze. "We can't be blank slates, but I'm glad you don't like all that purple either."

"It was a lot."

She laughed, and as I bent to kiss her, someone pounded on the front door. I groaned. It was likely only one person.

I curled my fingers through Cricket's. "That's probably Memphis."

Dread curled through my gut, but I led Cricket to the door.

I didn't answer fast enough. Memphis shouted, "Open up! I know you're not fine, you lying cocksucker."

Another squeak left Cricket. "She's worried about you."

I opened the door and faced my sister. She was a few inches shorter than me, but she towered over Cricket. Her hair was shoved off her face and her shaved sides were visible. She wore a plain white tee and jeans with rips in the knees. Her black boots only gave her more height.

Her vivid eyes went straight to Cricket, not missing our linked hands. "You brought a souvenir home?"

"Come on in." I stepped back and ushered her in. "I owe you answers."

"Clearly." Amusement danced in her voice, but I knew her better. She was startled and worry was setting in.

"This is Cricket. My wife."

~

CRICKET

. . .

His sister was so intimidating. I thought even my brother would cower before her. The hair, the clothes. If she drove a Harley here, I wouldn't be surprised, but I hadn't heard an engine. Where Maverick was easygoing, Memphis radiated a terminally pissed-off attitude.

She was mayor?

This town must run like a well-oiled machine. I couldn't imagine anyone crossing her.

Her gaze zeroed in on me and hardened. "What?"

The chill running through the room made me shiver. Maverick gave my hand a squeeze.

"I haven't told her about us yet, but she knows something's coming."

Memphis's eyes flared, and disbelief blanketed her face. "What? Fucking *A*, Maverick—what the hell were you thinking?"

"That she's the one I want." His instant answer and unwavering tone worked their way into my belly and sparked.

Memphis relaxed, but only slightly. "Since you know exactly what you did and what it means, I can see why you fucking ignored me for days."

And I thought my brother was overprotective. I didn't know what to do to defuse the situation, so I smiled. "Nice to meet you."

Her cool regard landed on me, and I tried not to squirm. I failed.

"She's got some balls," Memphis said flatly.

"She doesn't," Maverick replied in a matching tone. "I thoroughly checked."

Memphis made a retching sound. "Please, don't torture me. You're going to put me through enough in the next few days."

An ominous cloud hung in the air. I feared it'd suffocate me. "How bad is this secret?"

Memphis answered with levity. "Could be very bad for you."

"No one's harming her," Maverick said and tugged on my hand like he wanted to pull me behind him. "I promised her."

Shock raged through Memphis's expression. "Are you fucking kidding me?" She jabbed a finger in his chest. "Why didn't you just mate her and lock her down?"

"I'm not doing that to anyone," he said hotly.

She straightened and lifted her chin, challenge in her gaze. "Does she know she's only a rebound?"

"She's not a rebound," he bit out. "But yes, I told her about Astra."

I nodded as if that'd help. "It's the same for me. We met at my ex's wedding reception." I winced. That didn't sound like it'd help at all.

She threw her hands in the air. "Perfect. It's a match made in heaven," she said sarcastically. "I won't end up terminating my brother in front of the council. It'll be *fine*."

"Terminate?" She wouldn't be this upset if she just had to fire him.

Memphis flattened an *"I told you so"* look on him. "See."

"What I have with Cricket is special. She'll accept me."

"You'd better fucking hope so." She stomped to the door and spun. "I'm going to have to inform the council. You're fucking me over enough; I don't want them to think I'm hiding shit too."

"I understand."

She sighed. "Do you?"

"Yes, Memphis. But I believe in Cricket. There's something special between us. Something I don't want to lose. Maybe she's the reason I was driven to go to Vegas in the first place. Why I stayed in the hotel I did. Why I decided to walk around at the same moment she needed air. If Cricket isn't my fate, then I don't understand this world at all."

My chest bloomed with warmth like a cozy little fireplace was nestled next to my heart. He described exactly how I felt. The instinct that talked me into packing my bags and leaving my home to travel across the country to stay with a man I just met.

"You'd better hope so," Memphis said and then she was gone.

Maverick pulled me into his embrace. His breathing was even, but his heart was racing. Anxiety let the cold back in. Maverick was worried. He thought I'd reject him for what his family was.

"I just want to hold you tonight."

"Okay," I mumbled against his chest.

"Then, in the morning... I'll show you what I am."

I didn't know what that meant. Worst-case scenarios scrolled through my mind, but none of them made sense. Was the whole town full of criminals? Were penal colonies still a thing? A cult? But like... what would my limits be? Other wives? Ten kids and I'd put my foot down? Wash my clothing in the river? Was there even a river?

The questions exhausted me, and it'd been a long two days of driving. "Take me to bed, Maverick."

EIGHT

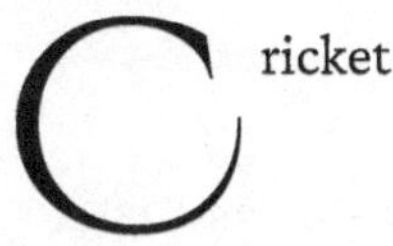

ricket

LAST NIGHT, Maverick made the bed while I showered. But when we crawled under the covers together, we didn't have sex. I was caged in his arms, like he was afraid I'd creep out in the middle of the night and run off.

I had no plans to. His embrace was exactly where I wanted to stay.

I opened my eyes to dark walls slashed with white. Astra had really liked shades of purple. The color in the bedroom was more of an eggplant and, by itself, was a lovely color. Deep and rich. But covering all the walls made a claustrophobic space. Same with the living room. Purple accents. I'd seen the pile of blinds. More eggplant. It was like Astra had challenged Maverick with the paint selections like she'd meant to pick an argument. Searching for a way to control him. But he'd allowed it and the insight told me a lot about what the relationship must've been like.

Peterson had used words to make me behave the way he wanted, and when I did, I became boring to him.

"Morning," Maverick murmured and rolled over to snuggle behind me.

"How do you always know when I'm awake? I haven't even moved."

"It's easy for me to tell."

"Because of what you're telling me later?"

"Mm." And the morning optimism was doused. Nerves fluttered through my stomach. We'd be talking, and I wanted to be dressed and fed before anything went down.

"Do you have food?"

"I cleared out as much of the perishables as I could before I left, but there's bread and peanut butter. Jelly that my brother's mate made is in the fridge. She's going to sell jellies and jams at the bakery and I'm her tester."

"There's a bakery in town?" I rolled up, hugging the sheet to my chest. If he made a move, I'd be helpless, but from the tension radiating from his side of the bed, I doubted he was in the mood. Or he would want to work it off.

Once we started, we'd be lost in each other. "I'll make some breakfast." I got out of bed and slipped my bra and underwear on. I was usually self-conscious about being naked in front of anyone, but Maverick watched like I was doing a striptease.

His gaze licked over my body, but he tossed me a T-shirt by his bed. "Wear my shirt. I like when you wear my clothes."

I'd only borrowed his shirt once to sneak to the bathroom on the night before we left Vegas. I tugged it over my head, and it swallowed me to my knees. Digging a pair of shorts out of my suitcase, I wondered if my outfit was really what I should be wearing for the big reveal. I stepped into the shorts and made a stop in the bathroom.

Feeling more myself than I had in a strange house last night after the run-in with Memphis, I went to the kitchen. "Want some toast?" I called.

"Yes, please. I might have some juice too."

The bread was next to the toaster. I found the peanut butter easy enough since whatever had been in the cabinets lined the counters, and the jelly in the fridge was labeled boysenberry.

"Your brother's calling," Maverick called from the bedroom.

"Tell him I'll call him back later today." I popped a couple slices into the toaster.

"He's going to think I have you tied up."

"Tell him I'll call him back after I use the safe word."

His deep chuckle could be heard from where I was waiting for the toast. "You're naughty."

Grinning, I turned around to look out the window. I hadn't seen Peridot Falls in the daylight. Thick trees surrounded his house and peaks of other houses were visible over some of the trees that were part of the landscape. The whole town was surrounded by woods.

Must be peaceful. Maverick had mentioned they were planning cabin rentals. These surroundings would be perfect for camping, and in a state with ten thousand lakes, there had to be one or two close by.

Shadows caught my eye, like something was moving in the trees. I squinted.

Maverick called from the bedroom. "He wants proof of life."

Since the toast was almost done and I couldn't take my eyes away from the trees, I didn't want to go to the bedroom. Maverick was still getting dressed, but Vaughn probably was demanding to hear my voice now.

I opened my mouth to yell that I was fine loud enough for my brother to hear through the phone when a large beast lumbered out of the tree line. I gasped, but I was frozen in place, my heart pounding.

Was I imagining—

It raised its big head and looked straight at me, yellow eyes narrowed and full of menace. Then it opened its mouth, baring long fangs dripping saliva and made a chomping motion in my direction. Then the toaster popped, and a scream ripped from my throat.

MAVERICK

I was by Cricket's side in minutes. She was on the floor, her head covered, sobbing.

"Cricket?" I dropped to my knees. I'd dropped her phone. Her brother would hate me, but I had to check on her. "What's wrong? What is it?"

She raised her watery gaze to me, her hands held at the side of her face like she was ready to cower in a second. "There's a monster outside."

Panic flooded my veins. Shit, shit, shit. There was only one kind of monster in Peridot Falls and I was supposed to ease her into knowing. "What'd you see?"

She pointed a shaky finger upward. "Is it—is it still there?"

I rose and checked my backyard. Nothing. I squatted again and cupped her face in my hand. I knew what she'd seen.

Shit.

I should've been the one to tell her, to show her. To get time to adjust to the concept of other creatures roaming among humans.

Her breathing was shaky, and she trembled. I gathered her in my arms and took her to the couch.

"Was I imagining it?" she asked in a weak voice. "Was I seeing things?"

I settled her on my lap and cupped her chin, gently meeting her wavering gaze. "No."

Her gasp was as unsteady as the rest of her. "What?"

"Did you see what looked like a dragon?"

She gave me an unsteady nod. Her eyes were pinched and the pained look reminded me of when we met.

It was time to tell her. The damage was already done. Perhaps I could salvage the rest of her sanity with the truth. If I didn't, she'd start questioning what she saw and her trust in me would degrade.

I scooted her around on my lap so she could face me. Her trembling had subsided, but her struggle to keep from crying gave her the shakes.

Cupping her face, I waited until she met my gaze. "I need you to listen to me and to trust everything I'm saying is the truth. I'll prove it soon enough when you're feeling better, but right now, I need to tell you everything."

Her brow furrowed, confusion mixing with her fear.

"I'm a dragon shifter."

Her confusion deepened and her lips formed a troubled line. "I don't get it."

I tilted my head toward the kitchen window. "What you saw out there was really a dragon. I can shift too. It's my other form and the other form of most people in Peridot Falls. We can shift, but we're very careful about how we do it." We prefer to shift at night when we can blend into our surroundings and be less obvious in case an unsuspecting human is nearby.

I didn't know who Cricket saw, but I wanted to wring their neck. Everyone in town knew the boundary lines between properties, and we respected them. What shifter was tramping through my backyard just when Cricket happened to be looking out the window? I didn't think Memphis would try to sabotage my relationship, but who else would know about Cricket?

Memphis said she would tell the council. Could one of the four shifters on the city council have spread the word?

"You turn into a dragon." She wasn't asking. The war was visible in her eyes. Disbelief battling against the reality of what she'd seen.

"There are other shifters." I let the whole story spell out. "Centuries ago, we were just dragons. Immortal and cruel, we didn't form attachments, and we didn't take mates or give birth very frequently. But then humans started populating the planet and became the dominant species. My ancestors made a deal with the powers that be—they gave up immortality to live among humans. All shifters. Wolves, mountain lions, bears, us. We became more humanlike. And really, there're not as many differences as you'd think."

She drew herself up, distancing herself from me

without getting off my lap. "So, you're saying there're not only dragons but other shifters?"

I nodded. "Not many of us live in populated areas. The other types of shifters can blend among humans better. They're driven to stay close to their packs, but they can move away and live in a big city, blend in. They might not be happy shifting less frequently or not at all, but once they're adults, they can control their natural aggression better than dragons. We need to stay among our people, and that's why I can't leave Peridot Falls."

She swallowed hard and glanced around the living room as she thought. Her forehead was tight and the lighter brown in her eyes dull, like she was fighting off a migraine. "I'm having such a hard time believing you, but..."

"I know."

"Peridot Falls is full of dragon shifters?" Her incredulous tone told me the disbelief was winning. Or she wanted it to win.

"Peridot Falls is my clan. We're named after gemstones, and each clan has formed its own town. Dragon shifters can move from clan to clan, intermate, or just move in if they're accepted by another clan, but it's different for me. My last name is Peridot because I come from the main line of the ruling Peridot family. Memphis's older, therefore she's the ruler." I lifted my shoulders. "Officially, she's really the mayor. We make it real to blend with humans."

She let out a scornful laugh and winced. "And here I was thinking it was so impressive she was such a young mayor and not the typical uptight person in the role."

I allowed myself a small smile, wishing I could heal her with more than humor, but we'd have to talk about that too. "You're the only one in town who doesn't think she's uptight."

Her shaky laugh turned into a half sob. She sniffled and swiped at her eyes. "I don't get this, Maverick."

I rubbed my hands along her thighs, and she didn't flinch. She looked so lost and hopeless, and I just wanted to wrap her in my arms and hold her all day, but I hadn't told her the rest. "There's more you need to know."

She huffed a strand of hair out of her face. "I'm afraid to ask what."

She should be. "It's against our laws to tell humans about us unless they are mates. It's a catch-22—we risk losing someone we want to mate by telling them, but we can't exactly mate them without them knowing. And only humans who are mates are allowed to know about us. Otherwise, there are penalties."

She swallowed hard, and I forced myself to continue.

"We cannot allow humans to live with the knowledge of us when they aren't part of the clan."

The information visibly sank in. She looked unsure for a heartbeat, then fear bled into the amber in her eyes, and it morphed into terror. "You're going to kill me?"

"No. I swore I wouldn't hurt you. And that's another thing. Dragon shifters can be terminated for breaking promises."

The line dissecting her brow returned. "You promised not to hurt me, knowing it could get you killed." She rolled her eyes and exhaled a noisy breath. "I feel foolish even saying this."

"I understand, but you're no fool. What we're talking about is life and death. I won't let any harm come to you, but in order to make that vow, I'm trading my life for yours."

She blinked and stared at me. More emotions traveled through her gaze until her expression settled on righteous anger. "You would die for me? Why would you do that?"

"Because no matter what, I don't want to force you to be with me. I want you with me because this is where you want to be."

She snapped her mouth closed and tears wavered in her eyes. "Maverick, I'm scared."

I held my arms open, not knowing if she would seek comfort from me. I wanted to do nothing but hold her, but I meant what I said. I wouldn't force her to stay with me. I had gone through the on-again, off-again routine with Astra so often, part of me was tempted to coerce Cricket to stay by my side by any means. But a better part of me healed, thanks to my time with Cricket, and yearned for a mate who wanted to stay with me and work through any issues without playing games or using manipulation. I wanted a healthy relationship like I saw with my brother and Briony.

She curled into my chest, her head on my shoulder. "I can't believe any of this," she mumbled into my shirt.

"I know. But when you're ready, I'll show you so you can know the real me before you decide."

"If I decide to go, you'll die." She hitched her breath. Her arms tightened around me.

"A price I'd gladly pay for your happiness."

She sat up abruptly, her hands pressing into my chest. "Don't you see? I can't be happy if you're hurt. This is worse. You'd be dead."

"Memphis would have to be the one to carry out the termination." And there it was. I'd gladly take the punishment so Cricket could be free, but I was condemning my sister to misery.

"That's awful."

"It's the way of our people."

"No wonder she wasn't thrilled with me." Sighing, she sank into me once again. "You were honest from the beginning, really. If we stayed married, I'd have to move to Peridot Falls."

I rubbed her back, enjoying having her so close to me, unsure how much longer I'd get this. "I kept using the word mate, hoping to lay some groundwork for us. We don't marry, Cricket. We mate. We bind ourselves together, and that bond will keep me sane. Dragon shifters need to mate by the time they're thirty-five because shortly after, the framework of our minds begins to degrade without a connection to a stabilizing force."

She pushed up again to meet my gaze. "Let me guess, death?"

"Termination. Same thing. Most dragon shifters get a grace period, but those of us from ruling families have to set the example. I have a few years, but, Cricket, if you stay, we'd need to mate. You'd be with me forever."

The brow creased again. "How long do you live for?"

"Our lifespans match humans, but we don't get sick like you guys do. We can heal ourselves, and the ruler is often gifted with extra healing abilities." I touched her forehead and trailed my finger down her cheek. "And those of us who are twins with the rulers get a little dose of it as well."

Understanding lit her gaze. "The migraine. You seriously cured it?"

"I wasn't sure I'd be able to. I hadn't tried until you."

A small smile graced her lips like she was touched. "And after sex?"

"I didn't want you to be uncomfortable because of me."

She let out a gusty sigh. "I should be upset, like, you should've asked permission, but I'm not. You aren't doing it now, are you?"

"I'll check with you from now on. If you plan to stay..." I didn't have it in me to ask the straightforward question. But my lungs froze, waiting for her response.

"Can you..." She pressed her fingers to her temple. "Is it bad for me to ask? I don't want a migraine to interfere with my learning. This is too important."

"Of course." I cupped my hands around hers and let my weak healing energy flow to her.

She studied me intently, scrutinizing every facet of my face, but the lines around her eyes relaxed. "Thank you. I suppose I should see the other side of you before I decide."

NINE

ricket

Was he really going to shift into that thing I saw earlier? Would he look at me with rage in the big orbs of his eyes? Would he glare at me like he wanted to sink those big teeth into my jugular and rip my throat out?

That terrified me more than everything he told me. The menace coming off the creature through the window was undeniable. I couldn't sleep next to Maverick if I felt the same from him.

We were outside at the edge of the trees in his yard. His nearest neighbors were at least a quarter of a mile away, and I could only see the black rooftops of their houses over the rows of bushes and trees between the properties. I rubbed my hands together, unable to get warm now that I was off his lap and free to remember the death stare from before.

Maverick took his shirt off, and while I'd never complained seeing his bare chest, I asked questions more out of nervousness than anything. "Why are you undressing?"

"Shifting into my dragon is a good way to ruin clothing."

He shucked off his sweats and underwear. Naked. I'd be more thrilled if I wasn't so scared of what was coming. Wrapping my arms around myself, I rubbed my hands up and down my biceps, like I was trying to start a fire.

"You ready?" His look was earnest, and no, I wasn't ready.

I swallowed hard and nodded. There was no way out but through. I couldn't turn back time, and as far as I knew, shifters couldn't either.

Maverick walked several feet away, the muscles in his ass flexing with each step. Was that why he was hot? Was it a shifter thing?

He'd said shifters could live in larger cities. Not dragons, but other shifters. What if I'd met some before?

I didn't have time to ponder the idea. Maverick started changing. A startled cry stuck in my throat, and I pressed my fingers against my lips to keep from shouting. I had screamed earlier from sheer shock and the thunk of the toaster had sent me over the edge. I was determined to be calmer now. But watching Maverick's limbs lengthen and his skin transform to green scales overlaid by a greenish-yellow hue, much like his eyes, made the idea of calm preposterous.

His face elongated into a snout similar to the one that had scared me before, and he grew. Larger than the other beast, but sleek. Lethal. And then he was done. He stood still, as if waiting for me to study him.

My focus was on his eyes. Was he a nasty creature who wanted to destroy me? Would I live a life of watching my back, being scared of my own husband?

When I looked into his eyes, I saw nothing but dread, like he was worried I would scream, like I would reject him and run off. There was no sense of menace, no cloud of hostility, only uncertainty.

He ducked his head, and I got the sense he was inviting me to approach him. Without thinking, my feet moved. Slowly, I drew closer until I was standing in front of him. Dipping his head down, he closed those brilliant eyes of his, and I missed seeing their shine. His sister's eyes were a lot like his, but Maverick's were still one of a kind. Reaching out, I stretched my fingers like I would in front of a fire. He was warm but not hot. He was... comfortable.

Clarity washed over me like the rays of the sun in the sky. He wasn't going to hurt me. He had an incredible, unique side to him that I was already starting to treasure.

A dragon shifter.

Who would have thought?

He already blew my mind in a way no other man could, but this made him even more special. He showed up in Vegas, and not only did he cross my path, but he put himself in my way and I ran right into him. Our meeting wasn't by chance. Peterson leaving me for my boss was as close to fate as I could get. Going to their reception sealed the deal. I was meant to meet Maverick, and I was meant to be in Peridot Falls with him.

I could figure the rest out later.

For the next several minutes, I ran my hands over his warm, smooth scales. "I can't believe how warm you are, but you're not hot. And wow, is that hardness from your muscles or the scales? Oh my god, a tail. Are those barbs on the end? Of course, you'd need them for fighting. Wait —do dragons fight? And these ridges on your back. Do you think there's any chance you're related to dinosaurs? Is that an insulting question?"

Maverick blinked at me and shook his head. My verbal barrage was amusing, judging from the humor in his eyes.

"This is amazing. Truly, it's really amazing, and I'm honored to be able to keep your secret." I pried my hands off of him when I really wanted to drape myself over his back, relieved that he was a friendly dragon. At least to me.

He bobbed his head, moving his snout out. Reading his body language, I stepped back.

He changed again, flowing from dragon to human.

"Does it hurt?" I asked.

Once he was the Maverick I was familiar with again, he shook his head. "No, it doesn't hurt."

"You can't talk when you're... him?"

The corner of his mouth tipped up. "I am him. No, I can't talk in that form. The heat is normal, but I am from a ruling family, so I can breathe fire."

"Cool."

He crossed to me in all his naked glory. "Do you really think so?"

Worry was etched in the lines around his eyes. Yes, I thought this was all cool, but he seemed like he was still scared. My early reaction was a reflection of what I thought about him and his people. "The other dragon looked mean, if that makes sense."

He frowned. "You sensed it wanted to harm you?"

"I certainly didn't feel like it liked me, but I only saw it for a couple of seconds."

"Did it have my coloring?" He brushed his hand down his body, but I knew he meant his scales.

"It was green, but it didn't have the sheen you do that's like your eye color."

He nodded like I had confirmed his suspicion. "Ruling families have a coloring over our scales that matches the jewel we're named after. Brighton, the ruler of Garnet clan, has a reddish-brown hue over her scales." He swept his arm to the side, pointing. "Garnet clan is the closest dragon shifter colony to us, that way. Emerald will have a brighter green than the natural forest green of our scales. Jade has a different green altogether, opal has a creamy translucence, and silver, well, you get the idea."

"Silver isn't a gemstone."

He flashed a grin. "But it is a precious material, and that is why Silver clan rules us all."

So interesting.

His smile faded. "But that doesn't narrow down who was in my backyard this morning."

"Are you upset with them?"

"It depends on why they were here." He put his fingers under my chin and tipped my face up. "I hate to pressure you, Chirp. Now that you know, I have to ask what you plan to do. My sister and the city council will need to know."

The city council must be important in the dragon shifter world. If Memphis wasn't really a mayor, then the council was likely not a true city council. And they must have some authority over Maverick.

I didn't want Maverick to get hurt. I certainly didn't want him to die. And above all that, I wanted to be with him. If it meant adjusting to living a life with beings I never knew existed until forty-five minutes ago, so be it.

"I don't plan to go anywhere."

The smile that broke across his face was more radiant than a thousand suns. "Really?"

"Really. You picked the wrong girl if you thought I would be scared away easily."

He chuckled, deep and relieved, and captured my mouth. He deepened the kiss and lifted me up. I wrapped my legs around him. He was already hard, his erection prodding against my bottom. But I was wearing shorts, and we were in the middle of his backyard.

He broke the kiss. "I'm ecstatic to hear you want to stay with me, but I'm so damn glad my sister won't have to kill me."

"No one's going to hurt you because of me. And don't worry, I understand the stress over a sibling—" Her gasp echoed across the yard. "My brother!"

MAVERICK

I GAVE Cricket privacy in the bedroom. She'd sprinted to the house while I got dressed, and by the time I got back inside, she was talking her brother down. He hadn't heard the confession—thank fuck. I hadn't hung up, but the phone had stayed in the bedroom while I'd laid out the truth of me and my people.

I couldn't blame him for being so worried. She'd screamed, and I hadn't cared about anything beyond her safety. The phone got left behind in the bedroom. At least

I didn't have to worry about Vaughn overhearing our conversation.

I wanted to bask in Cricket's acceptance of me, but not only did I have one obligation to fulfill, I also had an additional concern. Who the hell scared my mate?

I went into the bedroom to retrieve my phone.

Cricket lifted her gaze to mine while she spoke to her brother. "I swear I'm okay. They really have moose here, Vaughn. It just marched through the yard and startled me right as the toast popped up."

She'd already explained all that at least twice. "Tell him I'm sorry I dropped the phone, but I was worried about you."

Cricket nodded and spoke into the phone. "Did you hear that?" She pursed her lips. "We got to talking and forgot you were on the phone. I'm sorry."

Leaving her to deal with him, I grabbed my phone and went to the kitchen. Staring out the same window Cricket had seen the other dragon through, I called Memphis.

She answered, "I'm still so fucking mad at you."

"You don't need to be. She knows everything, and she wants to stay."

There was a beat of silence. "I won't feel better until you go through the actual mating ceremony."

"Give me some time. We're married, but I'll talk to her. We'll set a date."

Cricket's voice drifted from the bedroom, which reminded me of another minor concern.

"Listen, she's close to her brother. I'm sure he'll come up to visit a few times."

"See that he doesn't."

"At least once. He practically raised her. He's not

gonna let it go without checking out how she lives in Peridot Falls."

Memphis blew out a gusty sigh. "I can see why the past generations dissuaded human mates."

"It's definitely easier, but then we wouldn't be such a small, poor clan if our ancestors had branched out a little."

"You and Levi are certainly picking up the slack."

She sounded so salty I laughed. "You're next," I taunted.

Her snort was full of disagreement. "I'm holding out until the last second, and then I'll take someone in name only. I don't have time for someone else's bullshit."

If she had been in the same room as me, she'd have seen my smile fade. I'd been so content with Cricket the last few days, it was pure bliss. I'd known Astra most of my life and dated her for almost half of it. The turmoil, the ups and downs, wondering what was next. I was over it. In a short time, Cricket had shown me what a healthy relationship could be like. Yeah, I'd known her less than a week, but there hadn't been a stretch of that much time with Astra when we hadn't bickered.

I wanted that for my sister. I didn't want her to be alone with nothing but work in her life, and Peridot Falls made it hard to have anything else. She was restricted to the town to live and work in, and while she had dated, most of those guys had made her feel like she should be something different, someone different. Softer, more compliant, less foulmouthed. That wasn't her, and she deserved someone who accepted her as readily as Cricket had with me.

"If you toe the line of thirty-five, I'll never forgive

you." Then it would fall on me to terminate her, and I'd rather chop off both my arms than hurt my sister.

"Consider it payback."

"I wouldn't have risked it all with Cricket if I didn't think it'd work." Partially true. I had risked everything for Cricket. Hope for the best, plan for the worst kind of thing. Only the worst would've been pretty damn bad. "Hey, I didn't call you just to tell you we're in the clear."

I explained what happened this morning and my suspicions it wasn't an accident.

Moody silence filled the line. I didn't have to be in the same building as Memphis to predict how she was feeling. Irritation. *What now?* going through her head.

"I called a quick meeting with the council last night after I left your place. It was late but necessary," she said.

"Do you think they spread the word?"

"Absolutely. The main question then becomes, *Who would want to try to sabotage how well your human accepts you?* And you know which name comes up for me?"

My ex? "That doesn't make sense. She's mated to another guy. Why would she care what and who I was with?"

"Just saying. She was always kind of like that."

If Astra had waited in the trees for a moment, she could reveal herself to Cricket, hoping to catch her before I told her about us. That would be low but pointless. We were over. "I don't know, but she'd be smart enough to realize she wouldn't get punished for it."

A shifter who revealed our kind to a human who wasn't becoming part of the clan was terminated. But if Cricket accepted me, which she did, then there'd be no charges. If Cricket hadn't accepted me, it wouldn't have mattered because I would've had to tell her who I was anyway, and I'd already offered myself in place of her. Basically, the other dragon revealing themselves to Cricket was the loophole in our law.

And Astra worked in the law office in town.

"You need to decide what it means if it was Astra. And what it would mean for Astra and Cricket living in the same clan." Memphis's tone was grave. This was my problem, but one that would overflow to her.

"Shit." Astra could keep messing with my wife.

"Yeah."

I couldn't move to another town, and just because Memphis was my sister didn't mean she could run shifters out of city limits. Cricket was human, and any physical threat to her would cause more damage. She couldn't heal herself like dragons could.

"If it was Astra, I'll take care of it." It was close to a vow without saying the word. I wasn't fond of my ex, but I didn't want it to be her. We'd both paid for wasting years of our lives. Now that I was with Cricket, I was starting to hope Astra had found something as special with her new mate.

"You'd better," was all Memphis said before she hung up.

TEN

ricket

"I'm staying. That's all there is to it."

When I reached my phone after getting my reality destroyed, I had a dozen missed calls and several panicked messages from my brother. Guilty, I had called him back, hoping he hadn't called the police, the FBI, the CIA, and whatever other agency was out there. We'd been on the phone for several minutes, and I barely calmed him down.

"You can't just move. You just met the guy."

"And I'm in love. What can I tell you?"

"Someone in love doesn't scream like that."

We were cycling through a familiar part of our conversation. I didn't know what else to tell him. I'd extrapolated from my discussion with Maverick enough that if I told Vaughn, it was a death sentence—for him, for me, for Maverick, or for all of us, I didn't know, and I didn't want to find out. I couldn't imagine Maverick killing anyone, but there was a hard edge to him I found undeniably attractive.

And his sister... the steel lining her gaze told me enough. As for the dragon outside the window? Yeah, that looked like it could chew through humans.

"I don't know how many more ways to explain what happened." There were no other ways. "At some point, you just have to trust me to live my life."

Vaughn let out a heavy sigh, full of resigned disappointment. "You're moving across the country? Just like that?"

And there was the real problem. I considered myself a lonely soul before I met Maverick. I hadn't had many friends before I dated Peterson, and even fewer after. Once I was single, I realized I didn't have anyone close to me but my brother. I assumed it was different for him, but what if it wasn't?

Vaughn thrived on responsibility. Our parents had died, and he jumped right into raising me. Medical school, residency, he tackled it all with grim determination. His work was his life, but who did he have outside of me? His patients, the nurses, and his other colleagues weren't exactly people he went to have a beer with to talk over the struggles of the day and what he was really feeling deep down inside. Technically, he didn't do that with me either. He hovered over me like the parent of an only child. I knew little about his life, but he had made me the center of his. And now I was gone.

"I'm sorry. I wish I didn't have to move so far away."

"Why do you have to move?" Vaughn practically snarled. "Why can't he relocate?"

A loaded question I definitely couldn't give him the full answer to. "It's his work." Maverick had told me his duties working with the city, but I doubted my brother would buy the necessity of staying in Peridot Falls. "It's beautiful here though. His house is surrounded by trees, and it's so quiet, Vaughn. I can hear the birds from anywhere in the house, and I can sit out on the porch without the neighbors seeing me over a fence. There are no bars on anyone's windows."

"What would they worry about? Someone stealing a cow?"

A cranky joke was still humor. Was my brother finally softening and accepting my decision? "I didn't see many cows, but it was dark when we drove through last night."

So dark. The light pollution was minimal and during the final miles of our drive, I could look out the window and see an entire sky full of stars. The moon had been out, and there'd been a few clouds, but I could view the *entire* sky.

"Give it time," he said. "Before you decide for good, can you at least give it time?"

Of course, he wouldn't know the reasons why I couldn't. But he needed time more than me. "I'm not a prisoner here."

"I'm not so sure about that," he grumbled.

"I love you, Vaughn. I both love and hate how much you worry about me. But I'm fine, and I'm going to hang up now so I can go visit the bakery Maverick's brother's m—sister-in-law runs." I almost said mate.

"I'm calling you later today and randomly at different times in the next few days."

I rolled my eyes but smiled. I could ask for worse than having an overly attentive brother. "I understand. I didn't make this decision lightly, and I'm going to miss you." Tears pricked my eyes. I really would. He'd been my constant my entire life, and now we were over a thousand miles apart.

"You'd better."

We hung up, and I blinked back tears. Maverick came into the room and sat on the bed behind me like he guessed the conversation was done. Maybe he heard me say goodbye?

The dark town. The lack of streetlights. There were more than a few times he'd acted like he'd heard the entire conversation when I was on the phone with my brother. "Do you have supersensitive hearing and eyesight?"

"Yes." As simple as that.

I stared at my phone with its dark screen. "You really turn into a dragon." I'd seen it.

"Yes," he said quieter.

"That's trippy." It was all getting me so fast—the fright, his explanation, seeing him as an actual dragon. Mostly, the realization was sinking in that I would be living far away from the only family I had. "I was annoyed with my brother, but now I'm really sad."

Maverick gathered me into his arms for the second time today, only there was no explanation needed. He just held me. "We can travel to Las Vegas as often as you want."

Grateful he was trying to cheer me up, I shook my head. "I can't afford to go back and forth a lot. And now I have to find a new job." A lot of my duties could be done online. Truthfully, I didn't want to go back to being an accounts manager.

"I have my hoard."

I sat up and swiped the tears off my cheeks. "Hoard?"

"Dragon treasure." His grin was wolfish. "Gemstones—diamonds, rubies, emeralds, and anything else we find pretty." He lifted a heavy shoulder. "Which is pretty much all gemstones for us."

"Are you telling me you're rich and I am a kept woman?"

"We'll be okay, is what I'm trying to say. You have time to figure out what you want to do for work, and I'll keep helping my brother and sister build Peridot Falls up to be a comfortable community. We're small and isolated, and it's made it hard for the clan to earn a decent income and bring money into the community."

"I don't want to be a drain on you, your family, or your people."

He pressed a quick kiss to my lips. "You're not." He stood, pulling me up with him. "How about we visit Levi and Briony at the bakery?"

"I need to get dressed." That wasn't all. I'd be wandering deeper into a town full of shifters. Beings who weren't like me and may not like me, if the vibe from the dragon this morning was any indication, I wasn't sure I wanted to go anymore. But hiding in Maverick's house the rest of my life wasn't the answer either.

"Are you scared?"

"A little?" I gave his hand a squeeze. "Your sister wasn't thrilled to see me, and…"

He gave a firm nod, his gaze going hard. "I'm going to get to the bottom of what happened, but you're safe with me. I promise."

A spike of fear stabbed my chest. "If what you said about promises is true, you've gotta quit making them."

The corners of his eyes crinkled, and he leaned in. "I don't make any I don't plan to keep."

More fear piled into my heart. My life this week was entirely different from last week. My existence before meeting Maverick screamed of loneliness and boredom, but as I walked farther into the world of my shifter husband, I wished for some of it back.

~

MAVERICK

CRICKET WAS quiet on the short ride to the bakery on the other side of town. My brother and his mate had refurbished an old brick building into a bakery on the main floor with apartments above. They were working on erecting a place next door, but I hadn't heard what they'd planned to turn it into.

I liked the idea of cabin rentals with the office in the new building, and while Levi had asked to be included in more of the clan's decisions, to be put to work, I was looking forward to handling much of it but also working with him as much as I helped my sister.

I parked on the street in front of the bakery. The sign above the door read Kitty's Treats. "We're going to need to set a date."

Cricket blinked at me, and I didn't blame her. I had blurted it out with no context. Our Vegas wedding had been an almost impulsive act that was her idea. This was the closest I would get to asking her to mate with me. Shifters could exchange rings, but I didn't have the chance to prepare a jewel to go with the gold band on her finger yet.

"I should've waited until I had a chance to go through my hoard and let you choose a jewel for your ring."

She ignored the mention of jewelry. "Date for what?"

"To mate with me. To have a ceremony and a reception."

Her face brightened, and her expression fell. "I won't be able to have Vaughn at the ceremony."

"No." The ceremony glossed over the beginning of our people, where we were at now as dragon shifters, and how important taking a mate was. Nothing Vaughn could be present for. "But he could attend the reception. Memphis and I would have to talk to the townsfolk and make sure they're on their best behavior while he's here."

Hope sparked in her eyes. "So he'll be able to visit?"

She'd rather have her brother be part of our big day than a fancy jewel on her finger. I'd have to figure out how to make that happen. "I'll make sure of it."

Grinning, she got out of my pickup, and I walked with her into the bakery.

Levi was sitting at a table in the corner, reading something on his phone and sipping from a big white coffee mug. He glanced up and a broad grin stretched his mouth wide. "Look what you've been up to."

Briony popped out from the back room where she did much of the baking and, from what I understand, where Levi wasn't allowed because he had a sweet tooth and ate through too many batches of her goodies. "Maverick, hi. And you must be Cricket."

Cricket nodded but inched closer to me. "Nice to meet you."

Briony untied her apron and plopped it on the

counter behind the cash register. "Have a seat. I have a couple of pastries that I hope are perfect for newlyweds."

I glanced from Briony's enthusiastic bustling behind the counter while she readied our food to Levi's shit-eating grin. "You're taking this better than Memphis," I told him.

"She's going to be crusty no matter what. You and I are taken and everyone's going to be looking at her now."

True. I led Cricket to the table my brother was at and pulled her chair out.

Levi's brows drew together, and I grew defensive. "What?" I asked.

He shook his expression off. "I don't think I've ever seen you pull a chair out for a girl."

When he said it like that, it made me sound like a dirtbag. Heat wicked up my collar with Cricket's gaze on me. "I've been known to be a gentleman."

"I'll amend what I said. I've never seen you do it for no reason. Your charm always has a target, but the way you're doting on your wife is more like second nature."

Grudgingly, I got what he meant. Cricket should have nothing but the best treatment from me, and I didn't expect anything from her in return. With the rest of the town, I was usually making up for my sister's more abrasive attitude, trying to harbor good feelings where she'd inflicted damage with cutting remarks. And with my ex, I wished I could look back and think I'd been a better person, but we'd both been immature and selfish.

"I didn't mean to make it awkward," Levi said, flashing an apologetic smile toward Cricket.

"I can't speak for Maverick," she said as she sat, smoothing her hands over her fluffy hair. "But I don't mind having confirmation that he's not putting on an act. A lot of this still feels too good to be true."

Levi lifted his gaze toward mine, the big question simmering deep in his eyes. Briony doled out plates, nervously flicking her gaze across us before hurrying behind the counter to grab the drinks.

"Yes," I said, putting their mind at ease. "Not only does she know about us, but she's seen me."

Another big grin broke over his face. "That's good. Human mates are always touch and go for a little while."

"I wish it was all good news, but we had a bit of a run-in." I told them about what Cricket had seen.

"And you told Memphis?" Levi asked.

I nodded.

His lips pressed together. "And we're all thinking it's the same person?"

Cricket cut a glance at me, and I cursed myself for not telling her about my talk with Memphis. "I haven't talked with Cricket about my suspicions, but I've told her about Astra and what it was like between us."

"You're not holding back with any of it, are you?" Levi's tone was full of awe but also respect.

I rubbed my hand on Cricket's back, noting she hadn't touched her food yet. "She's been amazing about it, and she's too important to me to keep secrets."

Warmth and an emotion I couldn't identify swam in her eyes when she gave me a small smile. I tried to put myself in her place, and I couldn't. Learning about shifters. Getting married to a male and moving across the country with him on nothing but hope and a promise. And then meeting his family and hearing about his tumultuous past, all before she'd had a bite to eat.

"I have to say," Briony said, "I've been welcomed into

Peridot Falls, and I didn't think I would be, but it's nice to no longer be the only non–dragon shifter here."

Relief crossed Cricket's face, and her chuckle was shy. "I think I'm going to feel the same way." The smile the females exchanged hinted they'd become fast friends.

A part of me I hadn't known was tight relaxed. I didn't just want Cricket living with me, to become my mate, I wanted her happy. I wanted her to make a rich life full of people she adored. There was little I could do about her brother other than to order everyone in town to be careful when he came to visit.

CRICKET

I WANDERED around town with Maverick. This whole town could fit inside my neighborhood in Las Vegas. A few streets running north and south or east and west were lined with buildings that spread farther apart and deeper into the trees. I hadn't seen Levi's place, but he lived farther out of town than Maverick. A lot of the residents lived in the woods, and after seeing a couple of dragons, it made sense. More concealment. More room to roam as their other self.

We had looped around one of the neighborhoods close to downtown and were back on the main street the few businesses in Peridot Falls were on. "Do you fly?"

Maverick had been entertaining my questions all afternoon. "Yes. Flying is one of the most exhilarating things we can do." The next look he shot me was full of glittering promise. "Outside the bedroom."

Flutters erupted in my belly. Would there ever be a time one smoldering look from him wouldn't incinerate me from the inside out? I hoped not. "Noted."

"Would you like to see? Tonight?"

"Absolutely." Now that the initial fear was over, I'd definitely like to learn more. Would the greenish-yellow shine on his scales have a glow-in-the-dark effect? Would I be able to see him when he launched into the sky? Did they have some natural camouflage to blend in, like the *Predator*? So many questions and I hoped to get a lifetime with him to seek the answers.

"When it gets dark, I'll take you out." He hugged me into his side, and his voice got deep and growly. "But you have to stay close to me since you can't see as well at night as I can."

I let out a playful sigh. "How will I ever manage?"

We were walking past one of the more official cinder block buildings when the front door opened and Memphis walked out, followed by two older people. I was immediately locked in the tractor beam of their gazes. They looked grumpy, and I couldn't tell if they were always that way, if they just heard something that made them unhappy, or if it was me.

"Memphis," Maverick greeted. He inclined his head toward the other two. "Tina. Danielle."

The older female's mouth puckered. "And this is the human?"

I stiffened, trying not to take her reaction personally. Levi and Briony had been so warm I almost forgot I may not be a welcome novelty to anyone else.

"This human is to be my mate," Maverick said with a hard edge to his voice, a warning note ringing between us and them.

A mischievous light lit Memphis's eyes. She shoved her fingers in the front pockets of her jeans and adopted a casual stance, but wicked playfulness played along her lips. "So? When's the happy day?"

One of the females blanched like she was going to be sick. And the one that had asked about me soured until I couldn't tell if it was her expression or if she had just eaten a lemon.

"We were discussing that," Maverick said evenly. "I'd like her brother to join us for the reception. We'll need to prepare the town."

"What?" the sour one responded. "You expect us to put ourselves at risk and entertain a human who knows nothing of our kind and is no one's mate in *our* town?"

"Yes, Tina." Maverick's answer was hard and unyielding.

Memphis arched her brow. "Do you think that's a good idea?"

"I think if Deacon Silver was willing to do it, we should be able to."

"Deacon kept her father away from the main part of town," Tina said. "You live among everybody. I assume you'll want him to stay with you?"

The tension flowing through Maverick made him a steel pipe under my hands. "Our kind has entertained human mates since we made the deal with the powers that be. I don't think your ancestors would like to see us growing weak and lazy when it comes to how well we help our human mates adjust to our society."

The playful glint was back in Memphis's gaze. The other two drew back as if he'd slapped each of them.

"Lazy and weak," Danielle muttered. "I don't know

that our ancestors would approve of the ruling family insulting their council."

Maverick didn't flinch. His only reaction was his cool reply. "I don't think they'd approve of that council spreading the business of the ruling family around until someone felt the need to try to scare my mate away."

Irritation flashed through Tina's expression. Danielle looked confused.

Memphis snapped her fingers. "That's right. I have a leak in my council." She swirled her finger in the air. "I call a meeting."

Tina fluttered her fingers around the wide collar of her starched shirt. Her black shirt looked just as stiff. "You just adjourned a meeting."

"Sure did. Get back inside." Memphis spun and charged between them through the door.

We were shot one last glare from Tina before she followed. Danielle trailed quietly behind her.

"Whoa." I didn't know what else to say. I didn't want to be a disruption for Maverick or for his sister, but I didn't like how he was being treated.

"The more hostile one is Astra's grandmother, if that clears anything up for you."

The grandmother of his ex served on the council that happened to leak information after Memphis told them about me. "It clears a lot up, actually. Do you think it was one of them outside the window?"

I'd been trying not to walk through town, looking at people coming and going and wondering if they could turn into the dragon that was in the backyard. But no one who walked by looked at us as if they wanted to chop me into pieces. Their glances had been curious, stunned, and some happy ones that wished me and Maverick well.

Nothing like the vibe emanating from the dragon that stared at me through the window.

"I don't know," he said grimly. "We'll find out, and we'll figure out how to deal with them."

"They'll be punished for scaring me?" I was new to this world, but the only punishment Maverick spoke about was death. I hated to think I'd be responsible for someone's demise.

"It depends," was all he said. My reservations weren't eased in the slightest.

We continued to walk. I clung to his arm like I needed him in order to stay upright, but my mind was deep in thought. This world functioned so differently, yet it was the same. The drama might be more serious than my boss stealing my boyfriend away, but it was conflict. We walked past buildings and businesses that were struggling to keep their doors open, like so many towns in the rest of the country. People who tried to do the best for themselves and keep their loved ones safe.

I'd been in Peridot Falls for less than a day, but with each step, I could feel my roots growing into the ground and spreading. This place was where I belonged. With this man. Male. My mate. My dreams of meeting someone special and having a family weren't tabled after all.

This was the first time I had thought of having kids, and several more questions surfaced in my mind. "What will our kids be? Wait—do you want kids?"

His gaze landed on me, stealing my breath. The warmth and fondness in his eyes were smothered by pure delight. "Yeah, I want kids."

His expression said he loved the idea of children. Had he filed the possibility away as *not for me* like I had after my breakup with Peterson? The worst part about being single was the regret I had spent five years going nowhere. Would I invest five more years in the wrong man and end up alone again?

Maverick and his ex had circled around each other since they were teenagers. He might've been wondering if he'd spent his adult life waiting for the wrong person to come around. Had he been wondering if he'd have to put in another fifteen years with someone else and still face the chance of ending up alone?

But then he had to mate by thirty-five, so maybe not. Though he'd said nothing about whether he had to be in love with who he mated. Which made the way he looked at me feel even more special.

"Our children will be dragon shifters." He stopped and held both my hands in his. "Would that bother you?"

"Would I be the mother of dragons?" A horrified laugh sputtered out of me. "I'm sorry. I'm sorry I can't help myself."

His laughter rumbled between us. "You're not the first, and you won't be the last, to make that joke."

"I'd have to think about it, but my gut instinct says no, it won't bother me. Look at how you and your siblings turned out. You seem like amazing people."

"You haven't been around Memphis when she misplaces her keys."

I grinned, and we kept walking. Lost keys were a normal thing to throw a fit about, making her seem more relatable. I wrapped myself around his arm once again as we strolled. "It's a guaranteed thing?"

"Yes. A child will always have shifter traits, and a child with one dragon shifter parent will always be a dragon shifter."

"So if a bear shifter and a wolf shifter had a baby, what would happen?"

"They'd wait and see. But that's one reason dragon shifters must stay in dragon communities. We can't risk one of our children going to school with humans. And it's why our laws are so strict. We can't put someone in a jail cell when they can shift into a dragon and bust out. So you can imagine the issues with a human jail cell?" He shook his head.

The parameters of their world had a strict outline. Justifiably so. I could find happiness here, with Maverick, raising a family. I'd find a role within the community to help support their growth. And I'd respect their laws and hopefully they'd grow to respect me.

ELEVEN

averick

"HANG ON." I laughed as I trotted down the path in the darkness.

Night had fallen hours ago, and it was late, but she wanted to see me fly, and right now, there was nothing I wouldn't do for my mate. We hadn't set a date yet, but I wasn't bothered. The town needed time to adjust and accept her brother would be around for the reception. First, we needed to know when Vaughn could get here.

He'd been messaging her all day, but her phone had been silent for the last few hours.

I secured my hold where her legs were wrapped around my waist. She was on my back with her arms locked around my neck. Her exhilaration at the speed I jogged down the path and the dark night around us was palpable.

"This is so cool." Her voice so close to my ear made it hard to focus on the path and not stop to take her in the middle of the woods. "I keep wanting to be afraid you'll trip over something, and we'll both fall."

"I can see just fine."

There was a clearing with a small lake a hundred yards ahead. We were on my family's property, and not many others dared to risk Memphis's ire at being caught in one of her favorite flying spots. I still used this area all the time while Levi had found his own closer to his house. I could have gone there too, but I didn't want to be disturbed tonight.

Finally, we broke through the thickest of the trees. The lake wasn't a recreational spot. Half-dead trees stuck out at the edge of the waterline and reeds filled the spaces in and around them. There were fish in the lake, but not big enough to go through the effort of casting a line, and there was no good beach or rocky shore.

"I'm going to set you down carefully, but you need to stay in one spot. There's not really a path around the lake." I helped her down, loving the slide of her body against mine.

"Okay," she said breathlessly.

She was excited to see me fly, and I was like a five-year-old, pleading to show off my pet rock to the class. I stripped down, ignoring the way her gaze roamed over my body. I was nothing but shadows in the faint moon-light, but she was still looking, and that was all I regis-tered. If there was a decent spot to take her, my flight would have to wait. But I also liked the idea of fucking her in my brand-new bed. A good way to break in the house.

I walked several feet away and shifted, loving the

release in my body. The way my bones and skin stretched simultaneously and scales erupted over my body. Smells and colors grew stronger and more vibrant, and when I was finished shifting, I stretched for a second before launching myself into the air. I whisked through the night on the remnants of Cricket's awed gasp.

I soared through the air, keeping slightly above the treetops, and did a barrel roll before swooping back. I swung toward the surface of the water, dropping down to skim over the top and arcing up at the last second.

She let out a strangled cry that morphed into a delighted laugh. "Oh, I wish I could fly too."

As dragon shifters, we didn't like to take chances with our human mates. They were more fragile than us, less able to heal. Carrying them while flying was as treacherous as doing the fireman hold with a loved one down a steep flight of stairs. One trip and that could be the end of them.

The need to give my mate everything she wanted while keeping her safe warred inside me. Finally, I dropped down next to her and hunkered into a crouch. I jerked my snout toward my back, and her gaze jumped from my eyes to the ridges along my back.

I was three or four times the size she was. The bony scales running like armor down the middle of my back wouldn't be the most comfortable seat in the house, but I didn't plan to have her in the air for that long.

"You want me to hop on?"

I bobbed my head up and down.

She took a tentative step forward, putting her hand on her chest. Regarding me warily, she paused like her biggest concern was also for her safety. I didn't come equipped with seat belts.

I was about to shift into my human form and let her know it was okay if she passed on my offer when she scurried toward me. The feeling of her clambering over my body was new. Her athletic shoes were light scrapes against my scales, and the weight of her on my back was like a fully loaded hiking backpack, but while I was a dragon.

Twisting my neck around as much as I could, I silently implored her to hold tight to whatever she could. She settled over me and lay as flat as possible with her hands gripping one of the ridges.

Slowly, I flapped my wings before launching off the ground. The tall grasses fluttered and a few branches cracked, but I refused to lift off until she was done adjusting herself to the movement of my wings.

Once she was as secure as could be, I took flight, keeping low the entire time. I flew over the water to give her a forgiving landing spot should she fall. But she didn't slip or slide against my back. I made wide circles over the water, and her laughter rang into the night.

"This is so awesome!"

I didn't want to tempt fate. After a couple more rounds, I headed back to where I'd picked her up and landed. The way she dismounted was more of an awkward slide that would've made me chuckle had I been in my other form. She was too damn adorable.

When she stepped back, straightening her shirt that had gotten pushed up during the dismount, her face was flushed and her smile wide. "I never knew that was a bucket list item. That's way beyond a bucket list item. It's like something out of a fantasy—who would believe I've ridden a dragon?" Her eyes went wide, and she waved her hand like she was erasing a chalkboard. "I won't tell anyone. But, seriously, that was out of this world. Like, who gets to do that?"

I shifted back, letting my body compact itself into the shape of a human. I rolled my shoulders, unaccustomed to the extra weight while flying but planning when we could do it again. "I want to keep fulfilling your dreams— even the ones you don't know you have."

She let out a satisfied sigh. "Oh, Maverick. You've been doing that since we met."

"We're only rounding out our first week. I plan to have a lot of time with you." I tossed my clothing back on. I was impatient to have her back in my arms.

"It's been a hell of a week."

I crossed to her and put my hands on her shoulders, stroking my thumbs over the thrumming pulse at the base of her neck. "It's been the best week of my life."

"Maverick." The thick desire in her voice was the only prompting I needed.

I helped her climb on piggyback style, and I sprinted through the woods to my house. She held on tight, but there was an urgency in her embrace that hadn't been there when we'd gone out for the night. She needed this too. The connection, the affirmation, that this week was only the beginning. The beginning of us and the start of a wonderful life together.

I didn't put her down as I slammed through the door and kicked it shut behind me. I didn't stop until I was in the bedroom and could flip her on the bed.

I took her shoes off and tossed them in the corner. "This is going to be the first time between us when you know who I truly am."

She sat up, propping herself on her hands behind her

while I worked on dragging her shorts and underwear off. "I knew who you truly were when we first had sex."

Her words were humbling. I'd found a human mate, and she'd accepted me. We'd been through more real life than I had ever had in my past flimsy relationship. This woman was mine, and I couldn't wait until it was official.

Our arms tangled as we yanked each other's shirts off, and before I climbed on top of her, I stripped out of my sweats and shoes. Finally, I was naked with my woman.

I was stretched over her, her warm body beneath me. She cradled me between her legs and it wouldn't take much adjusting for me to thrust inside of her. Her arousal was strong and she'd be ready for me, but I wasn't in a rush. She was the most valuable thing in my possession and I would treasure her.

"I hope it's not too soon to tell you I love you."

Her lips parted, and she cupped my face in her hands. "I was afraid you'd think it was too soon if I told you I loved you. But I do. I didn't think it was possible to fall for someone so fast, but it was impossible not to fall in love with you."

My grin was overpowering but not as strong as my need to taste her. I claimed her mouth and rocked my hips against her. My erection was wedged between us and pressed against her hot belly. Soon. I wanted her ready for me.

When I ripped my lips off hers to kiss my way down her neck, she squirmed under me. She tangled her hands in my hair and gently pried my face away from her. "There's one thing I haven't done to you and I'd like to."

I frowned at her timid tone. I was about to ask what

she meant when her gaze dropped to where our hips lined up.

"You want to blow me?" I'd fucking love her lips on my dick, to see her mouth wrapped around my cock while I tried not to gag her. But it wasn't quite the romantic connection I had envisioned tonight.

Yet who was I to deny my mate? I rolled to my side, taking my weight off her. She bit her lip and scooted around until she was between my legs. I buried my heels in the mattress, my knees bent, and the view of her kneeling between them with her breasts on full display and her hand wrapped around my erection was an image I'd never forget. She was beautiful with her constantly tousled hair and her flushed cheeks.

Almost shyly, she descended on me, wrapping her pink lips around the tip and giving me a tentative lick. Her tongue could have just as well been a downed wire. My hips shot up, and I unintentionally stuffed myself farther into her mouth.

"Shit, sorry," I said through clenched teeth, stifling the sheer pleasure shocking my system.

She whipped her head up. "Oh no—it's fine. Are you okay?"

"More than okay. I'm not going to last long watching you lick my cock."

The bloom in her cheeks matched the swell of her arousal. She dipped down again, and this time I was a rock. A desire-ridden boulder that wouldn't move in order for her mouth to stay on my shaft.

I'd never experienced pleasure that bordered on sheer torture. She swallowed me down and ran her tongue back up.

"Fuck, Cricket."

She hummed, and my hips kicked again. "Sorry." I couldn't have her stop. It'd kill me.

She continued the humming, and I rocked my pelvis in time with her bobbing. Her hot tongue was all over, swirling. Pressure coiled and increased until I was a smoke stack waiting to blow.

"Cricket—"

She doubled down. I sputtered, trying to warn her, but it was pointless. She was a woman on a mission, and when I roared my climax, released into the wet depths of her mouth, she sucked until I was wrung dry.

When I went limp, she lifted her head and prowled over me to lie by my side. "That was intense."

"Hell yeah, it was." I struggled to catch my breath, but the picture of her swallowing me down couldn't be forgotten. I wasn't done yet. "Now climb on top."

She popped her head up. "So soon?"

Growling, I lifted her to straddle me. She sank onto me, needing no more preparation. She was dripping wet, and I was coated in her before the first stroke.

I didn't give her a chance to ride me. I took over, lifting her up and down. "I want to claim you." We hadn't talked about it yet and I couldn't bite her until she knew what it meant.

"Do it." Her hands were pressed into my chest, her fingers spread.

I ripped my gaze off her bouncing tits. "It means I bite you."

Interest darkened her eyes. "Do it."

"You don't know—"

"I trust you," she whined, leaning into me. She was close, her body greedily gripping mine.

Flipping us, I slammed her back into the mattress and

continued thrusting, angling my hips to hit the spot I knew drove her the wildest. The more she writhed, the closer I got to a second orgasm.

I was crazy for this woman, and she'd wear my bite. When she crested, I licked across the spot at the base of her neck before I bit. The ecstasy devastating my body increased and her body clamped on to mine. My grunts were lost in her yells. I poured inside of her and when she grew weak from coming, I released. The last thing that would completely make her mine was the ceremony binding us together, and if she said she wanted to do it in the morning, I'd be up at dawn.

~

CRICKET

I FEATHERED my fingers along my neck. The spot he'd bitten tingled, and it was like a line traveled directly from the base of my neck to my core. After being with Maverick, I knew I could come again, but I enjoyed lounging in his arms. We were both still naked with no covers on us.

"Does it always feel like this?" I couldn't quit touching it.

"I don't know. I've never claimed anyone."

I craned my head to look up at him. No humor was written on his face. "Really?"

"I never got around to it with Astra. That says a lot."

"You can only claim one?"

"Yes. Not all mates claim each other. It's a deep longing to make sure everyone knows you're mine."

"I am yours." I snuggled into him. "So when should we have the ceremony?"

"When Vaughn can make it."

"You mean that?" How sweet and considerate could he be?

"Absolutely."

"What do I do?" I trailed my fingers over his abdomen, marveling at the taut muscles underneath his skin. "I know I'm new here, and I'd like some time to settle in, but what's the job market like?"

When I peeked up, his lips were in a firm, flat line. "Dismal. We are working on it, but we don't have many businesses or shops in town."

I rolled up to an elbow. "I was an accounts manager, but my background was in business. I noticed there wasn't a little store."

"There's the grocery store. It has the essentials."

"Exactly, but what about the fun stuff? Crafting supplies, different clothing, I don't know... like a dollar store."

An eyebrow ticked up. "You should bring the idea up to Levi. He's been taking queries about what to put into the building they're planning next to the bakery. I thought maybe the cabin rental office, but it wouldn't need much space."

Excitement sparked inside of me. I wouldn't be the boss, but it would be fun to be in charge of a project. And to not be hindered by the complicated bureaucratic process of the office environment. Ideas pitched to different managers, then waiting on their opinions, and having one project get pushed aside for a higher status client. I'd found the process so frustrating, self-centered boss aside. I wanted to work. I wanted to come home to a place that was mine, to a family, but also contribute to my community. In Vegas, it was easy to get lost in the daily grind. But in Peridot Falls, I could be somebody, not just an accounts manager or Maverick's mate.

He threaded his fingers through mine. "But before we call him, I'd like to decide on a color for the blinds. I don't mind anyone seeing me fuck my wife, but I think you'd have a problem with it."

Alarmed, I sputtered. I'd forgotten about the lack of window covering. Then I laughed. Grinning, I glanced around at his half-painted room. "After the dark eggplant, the white will be nice and open. And Briony mentioned the lady who runs the café is an artist. I'd love to see some of her work."

"We'll go there for breakfast. You can see her art, and maybe Memphis will meet us there."

The thread of worry was in his voice. I brushed my thumb along the side of his hand. "This council? You're worried about the trouble they're giving your sister?"

"I don't know. Not the entire council, but something wasn't right about Danielle and Tina's reaction and the way you were welcomed into town. Danielle might've been concerned about a human in town, but Tina's Astra's grandmother. My relationship with Astra wasn't right, or we wouldn't have had the troubles we did. So I don't know why she'd be upset or why someone needed to frighten you."

I rested my head on his chest, wishing we had no other worries but how to brighten several rooms of purple paint. But we had each other, and he had his family. I had Vaughn, but there would be distance between us like there'd never been before.

I had a hard time not thinking about Vaughn. My

brother saw things in black and white, and I'd love to get his opinion on what was going on, but I couldn't tell him. For his safety, he couldn't know. So, I'd settle with being satisfied he could attend the reception after our mating ceremony, and after that, I'd have to deal with the heart-break of not getting to see him very often.

I felt like I was trading one relationship for another, both equally important to me. Maybe Vaughn could find someone that made him as complete as Maverick made me. Then I wouldn't feel like the worst sister in the world.

TWELVE

averick

CRICKET WALKED THROUGH THE DINER, studying the artwork on the walls. Memphis and I were bent over the remnants of our breakfast. I had encouraged Cricket to order the strawberry and cream cheese stuffed French toast, and like I thought—she said it was her favorite. There weren't too many other customers in the diner this late in the morning, but Memphis spoke so low only I could hear.

"I don't know what her problem was," Memphis murmured. "I called the four council members together and told them about Cricket. Even though I stressed you haven't told her about shifters yet, two were thrilled you were settling down."

I nodded. It didn't matter the clan, the entire town breathed a sigh of relief when one of the ruling family was mated before their thirty-fifth birthday. Our punishments rocked the foundation of our society harder than others and mating was one large obstacle out of the way.

The four council members had been in place for years. I'd like to think those who'd known my parents and had watched me grow up were thrilled I had found my special someone. They did have the typical shifter anxiety over human mates, but they'd hope for the best.

"Anyway," Memphis continued. "Danielle was probably uptight because Tina was salty as hell. Tina always gets her way, and she was the one who brought up terminating Levi for that situation. The others followed her lead. I don't know what her problem is now, but she wanted you and Astra together."

"Why? Astra and I weren't happy. Wouldn't a grandmother rather have her grandkids be in a stable, loving relationship than a tumultuous one where we broke up every other month?"

Memphis shrugged and took a swig of her ice water. "You would think, but that family's always been different."

Since meeting Cricket, I was coming to terms with Astra and how things had been between us. My ill will toward my ex for the way she'd manipulated me for years before dropping me like a hot stone and mating someone I didn't think she had even talked to was fading to nothing. I'd rather she was as happy as me. I'd feel better if she found someone she was as comfortable with and crazy about as I was with Cricket. I was a happy male, the obnoxious type that wanted everyone around him to feel just as good.

Cricket wandered back over, a content smile on her

face. She slipped into the booth next to me. "I really like her watercolor of the sunset over the trees. I think that'd look good in the bedroom, over the bed. What do you think?"

Memphis's gaze was on us, dancing back and forth between me and Cricket. I could read her expression clearly. She hadn't seen this interaction between me and Astra. My ex had demanded, we'd argue, and then she'd get her way or we'd break up. A simple *what do you think?* hadn't been part of the conversation.

Out of habit, I said, "What do you want?"

Cricket's gaze strayed to the painting. "I like it, but I want something we both can enjoy. If you think it'll go good somewhere else in the house, we can buy it, or I can just admire it every time we come to eat until someone else buys it."

Memphis sat back, her expression flummoxed. "And if he says no, you're just gonna let it go? Easy as that?"

Cricket nodded, seemingly clueless about why we were having an in-depth conversation about one decoration in an entire house. "I trust we'll find something we both like."

Memphis turned her attention to me, a dark brow arched. Then she pushed her plate over and scooted to the end of the booth. "I'll buy the painting for you. My mating gift to you."

I was stunned, but Cricket's eyes widened. She laid her hand on her chest like she was touched. "You don't have to do that. Maverick hasn't even said if he wants it."

"Maverick honestly doesn't care," my sister said, and she was accurate. "But he's mentioned that painting before, so I know he likes it. You want it though, and that's enough for him."

"True," I said.

"You two have that twin thing going on, don't you?" Cricket said, grinning. "Did you used to have your own language too?"

Her question was innocent and her insight was accurate, and her tone was filled with both fondness and curiosity. Yet again, she behaved so different than my ex. Astra's jealous streak had been a mile wide, but its epicenter was my relationship with Memphis.

I might as well answer honestly and learn if there were going to be any issues sooner than later. "We often know what the other's thinking or feeling. It can be unnerving to some people that we don't need to talk before we come to a decision, or that we can be overprotective with each other because we know what their interests and weaknesses are."

Cricket nodded thoughtfully. "My brother and I are a little like that because we had to grow up closer than a typical brother and sister." She gave me a wry smile. "Which you got to be a firsthand recipient of. But the communication thing, that's cool. It must be pretty special."

"His ex found it annoying as hell," Memphis said bluntly.

"I suppose it can be intimidating." Cricket twined her fingers in mine, but not in a territorial way. More like a show of support. "I'll make sure I don't get to the point where it bothers me. Any inadequacy your connection makes me feel is likely due to a lack of communication in my relationship with Maverick. It'd be a sign we need to work on us."

Memphis stared at her for a moment, then blinked. "You seem like you should be such a timid little thing, but you're not. I can see why my brother fell for you so hard."

Cricket beamed, and relief washed through my insides. Other than Memphis's first stunned reaction when I brought a mate home, she'd been open-minded but neutral. This morning was the first real sign of acceptance.

My time line with Cricket was moving at warp speed, but I wouldn't change a thing. I hadn't admitted how important it was for me that my mate and my family got along, not merely tolerating each other, but valuing their respective places in my life. It was a gift I wouldn't take for granted. Nor would I forget I was asking Cricket to walk away from a big part of her only surviving family member's life.

CRICKET

I WANDERED out of the diner tucked into Maverick's side while he chatted with Memphis about when he'd officially be back in his office. His sister slid on a pair of aviator shades, which only added to her aloof *don't mess with me* persona. She was dressed much like yesterday, and her black boots looked like she could tread through a pasture full of spikes while my athletic shoes were only good for an asphalt bike path.

I liked her. We hadn't had much time to talk or get to know each other personally, but she was protective of Maverick, and that was all I needed to know. She wasn't hostile toward me, and I didn't know if we'd ever be close friends or if she was close with anyone other than her twin, but that was okay.

Memphis turned, probably to say *see ya* and go back to the city hall building she worked in, but she closed her mouth, her lips forming a troubled line.

"Shit," she said under her breath.

I twisted around to look, forgetting to be discrete but if something unsettled an obviously strong person like Memphis, then I wanted to be prepared for what was coming. All I saw was another couple. An older male with a bushy salt-and-pepper beard and longish hair, with the same gray as his facial hair. He was attractive in a bushy mountain man sort of way, but his expression would scare anyone away from talking with him. His dark brows drew when his gaze landed on Maverick and he stiffened. The female next to him was an attractive brunette with her hair pulled into a high ponytail and a sheath dress fitted over her curvy body. If she'd worn pointed heels, she'd ooze sex appeal, but the hiking boots made me do a double take. At first glance, the couple looked like a mismatched pair, but they worked. Her sexiness offset his hardness, but the hiking boots tied her into his lumber-jack outfit of rugged jeans, plaid shirt, and thick solid boots.

"Astra. Jack." Maverick dipped his head in a cautious greeting.

This was Astra? I wasn't sure what I expected, but someone close to my age with a thousand times the hotness I had, wasn't it. She looked like she could be Maverick's mate, not me.

But I recalled the purple walls and the gaudy blinds and the way Maverick described their tumultuous rela-tionship. Instead of being jealous, I was relieved this initial meeting was getting over with sooner rather than later if we were to live in the same town together.

"Maverick," she said in a flat tone. She was holding hands with her mate, but her knuckles were white. "How are you?"

Her inquiry was almost robotic, and Maverick's answer was just as wooden. "I am well. And you?" His gaze jumped between the two of them like he was letting both Astra and Jack know he wasn't just asking after her.

"We're well," she answered, a little more relaxed than her initial words. "I hear congratulations are in order."

Maverick's hand tightened around my shoulder, more like a reassuring squeeze, but whether it was meant for me or him, I didn't know. "This is Cricket. We met when I went to Vegas."

Taking a chance, I stepped out of Maverick's hold and extended my hand. "Nice to meet you. Astra, right?"

She warily shook my hand, her grip solid but not punishing. I switched my handshake offer to the male at her side.

"Jack? Did I get that right?"

"Yes." His voice was rough, like he barely used it. His grip was firm but polite and he studied me, almost like we were kindred spirits. Two people who had each fallen in love with someone and those two someones had a matching set of baggage.

I stepped back to Maverick and hooked my arm through his elbow. The tension was ripe between us and them and growing. I had to do something. I doubted any of us wanted to live on alert that we'd run across each other again. "I'm happy we got this first meeting out of the way. I'd hate for it to get awkward."

Memphis snorted a chuckle. Jack arched a brow.

Astra lifted her chin, a hint of defiance in her eyes. "To answer your questions, since I'm sure you've heard of me, and you'll hear more. Yes, my relationship with Jack is real, and frankly, I'm tired of everyone thinking I mated him out of spite."

"You'd never do anything out of spite, Astra," Memphis said, her lips quirked.

Astra smacked her lips. "Fair. But Jack never came to town enough for me to get to know him. I didn't even think he knew I existed until he hired me to notarize some documents. Then he asked me to give him some interior design tips."

The words were out of my mouth before I could stop them. "Did you paint his place purple?"

Maverick made a choking sound, and Memphis had to turn around with her knuckle against her mouth. Astra and her mate stared at me. My heart hammered, and they could all probably hear it. How badly had I crossed the line? I didn't want to make an enemy of Astra. We didn't need to be friends, but we had to exist together in a small town, and I'd probably ruined it.

Finally, Astra exchanged a look with Jack. "Told you."

When we all turned our attention toward Jack, he spoke. "She warned me I'd know she was upset with me if she made me paint every wall in the house different shades of the same color."

"Careful, man," Maverick said, holding back a laugh. "You'll be covering the deepest shade of purple with so many coats of primer you'll never want to lift a roller again."

Satisfaction gleamed in Astra's eyes. "We had a fucked-up relationship."

"Yes, we did," Maverick said solemnly.

A voice I recognized from yesterday barked from across the street. "Astra. Now is your chance."

Her grandmother marched across the road, gray dress swirling around her legs with more movement than yesterday's clothing had, and her expression was more puckered than before.

"Chance for what?" Astra frowned, just as startled and confused as the rest of us.

Tina jabbed a finger in my direction. "Challenge her."

Astra recoiled. "Why would I want to do that?"

Maverick edged in front of me, putting himself between everyone and me. "You were the dragon in the backyard."

This time all heads swung in his direction.

Tina raised herself to her full, diminutive height and peered down her nose at him. "You were supposed to mate my granddaughter. She was supposed to have babies in the ruling family."

"Um," Memphis said as she crossed her arms. "It's going to be my kids who are the next ruling family."

Tina's lips curled, and disdain dripped off every word. "We all know you are never going to take a mate. You can't even keep a guy long enough to call him a boyfriend. And you rarely leave town. When you did, you messed up your only chance to mate over the male."

I was confused as hell, and I wasn't the only one. Astonishment crossed Memphis's face, and her mouth dropped open. I didn't have to know her long to realize I was witnessing a rare reaction. "Ronan Jade was already taken before I traveled to Garnet River. And I date. Not that it's any of your business until I turn thirty-five."

This was about babies and children. Astra held no ill will against me, but my relief was drowned out by fear.

Her grandmother saw me as the person who ruined what could have been. She couldn't see the truth. Maverick and Astra had spent a decade of their adult lives together without even a claiming bite. Their union wasn't going to happen.

And now he was mine.

"Astra, she's a human." Tina's gaze grew frantic. "You can take her."

Astra's mate angled his body to block her, much like Maverick had done for me.

Undaunted, Astra sidestepped him and put a quelling hand on his shoulder. "Grandma, I'm in love with my mate. I have no need to challenge anyone. I wish Maverick and Cricket the best, and knowing we're both happily mated makes me feel like I didn't waste half my life with the wrong guy."

I could be touched by her words later. The tension running between everyone in our little group spread through the town. People lined the sidewalk on either side of the street, watching us. I flattened a hand against Maverick's back, and it was like I touched a battery waiting to explode.

Memphis marched forward, putting herself in line with Tina. "There's no problem between my brother and Astra and their mates. But you and I? We have a problem."

"What law, exactly, did I break?" Tina's tone was snide, righteous. She'd made this scene, and she was getting away with it.

I knew so little about these people and their laws, but the only punishment was death. I didn't want to watch anyone get killed today. Nor did I want Memphis to have to do it. She was a hard female who loved her family, but I sensed she was isolated and alone because of her position. A death on her conscience would only add another layer between her and everyone else.

"I'll think of something," Memphis hissed.

Tina's gaze turned imperious. "The only thing I'm guilty of is wanting what's best for my granddaughter."

"You revealed yourself to a human," Memphis said.

"A human that is already married to a dragon shifter. You said yourself hours before that girl saw me your brother was going to tell her about us. Why is she staying in Peridot Falls if no one's been informed of the danger of shifting around her?"

"You were trying to scare her away, and we all know it. You've been tampering with the emotions of the ruling family and plotting a takeover from the inside out."

Alarm flashed in Tina's eyes before she lifted her chin and slowly started unbuttoning the top of her long gray dress. "Prove it. You've been leading this town with a nasty attitude. It's time to call you on it."

Astra stepped forward, patting her mate on the shoulder as if to tell him to hold back. "All you wanted was for me to have Peridot babies?"

"I wanted to breed stronger leaders. Our kin has served the Peridot ruling family for generations, and when you and Maverick started dating, I thought *finally*. Finally, we will take our rightful place in this clan. It was all coming together and then you mated *him*."

"I love him. All those times you pressured me to get back together with Maverick was so I could breed us into the Peridots?"

Maverick rocked on his heels, and my heart went out to him. He and Astra had been manipulated for years.

They each could've found their partners earlier without the interference of Tina.

Memphis fisted her hands, but she didn't undress. "You tried to have me kill Levi to disrupt me."

"You were too weak to do even that," Tina sneered. "The council listens to me, not you."

Memphis ripped her shirt off. "Not for long."

THIRTEEN

averick

I COULDN'T BELIEVE what I was hearing. One of the shifters who was supposed to have the clan's best interest in mind confessed to having manipulated me and my ex since we'd been kids. And she'd likely kept Memphis busy with bullshit clan problems so she couldn't find her own mate.

Memphis wasn't officially challenged, but Tina needed to face the consequences. Years of tampering with our relationships, plotting against Levi, topped off by trying to frighten my mate away from me, couldn't be ignored. Memphis was in a shit position. Being a jackass wasn't necessarily a reason to be killed, and if Memphis was facing one of the city council members, she'd need an ironclad reason for harming Tina. The ruler functioned with the council members as a sort of checks and balances system, and when the check slaughtered a balance on Main Street in front of the entire town, it could have serious repercussions.

And there was no time for Memphis to consult the rest of the council. She'd terminate now, ask for forgiveness later, but perhaps that was best. She needed to establish her dominance if the council had been listening to Tina over her.

I didn't want Cricket to be around this fight, but I needed to be here for my sister. Memphis was already undressed. She faced off with Tina, unwilling to be the first to challenge. If Tina made the first move, she'd be signing her own death notice.

"Grandma, don't do this." Astra's attempt to talk down her grandmother only seemed to embolden the female. Tina was enraged and the evidence of her feelings was right in front of her. Astra and her mate. Me and Cricket.

"Tina, it was never your decision to make." I had to be able to talk some sense into Tina before she shifted. Once she changed into her dragon, she'd be seen as more of a direct threat to Memphis. My sister would have to respond. "You said your family has been serving for generations, but what if you chose the wrong time to interfere? You know there's always an aspect of fate in our pairings."

Tina was nude, in the middle of town, and ready to shift. Her gaze went from Astra to Cricket. Comprehension dimmed her rage as she understood what I meant. What if it wasn't Astra and me who were supposed to be together but our respective children?

"It should have been you two. I saw it when you were children."

More like she'd also realized that it wouldn't have mattered if my child fell in love and mated Astra's kid if Memphis was still around. She wanted to interfere with the born leader of the clan and replace her with someone who was easier to manipulate.

"Grandma—"

Tina cut her hand through the air. "Enough. I've had enough of this." Her intense gaze settled on my sister. "I officially challenge you."

And there it was. She hoped to defeat Memphis, leaving me as ruler. If Astra and I couldn't be mated, then she wanted to open the path for our children to get to the top. Perhaps she hoped Astra's parents would step in where she left off and encourage our children to mate, finally bringing Astra's bloodline into the ruling family.

"Then fuck you, Tina," Memphis said, resigned. She morphed into a dragon, identical to mine.

Tina shifted, her dragon smaller and dulled compared to Memphis. Behind me, I felt Cricket's flinch, confirming Tina was the dragon she'd seen.

"Grandma," Astra whimpered. Jack wrapped her in his embrace, almost as if he was afraid she'd dive in to defend her grandmother.

Tina prowled to meet Memphis. A display of power. When the limbs lengthened and a tail grew, it could affect balance. Total power play and a mental game that wouldn't work against my sister. We grew up doing it to each other when we trained together.

I was torn between standing in front of Cricket to protect her from battling dragons and flying objects that occurred during the fight and cocooning her in my arms to ensure she was okay.

The need to touch her won out. She cowered behind

me, her expression distraught and fear shining in her eyes. "I'm so sorry. All of you have been manipulated for so long that it has to hurt."

Cricket wasn't scared for herself. She was upset about us, and she understood what Memphis was doing would be hard on the clan, especially my sister and, of course, Astra.

My ex buried her face in her mate's shoulder as if she couldn't watch while he kept his resolute gaze on the fighting dragons.

The roars of the females echoed off the buildings and thundered down the street, drowning out the faintest drone of a car engine. Hopefully, whoever was driving this way stopped a couple blocks from the fight.

Tina was a wily opponent. She was older, but she also had a lot of experience and had kept in excellent shape, but she was no match for Memphis. My sister had grown up being trained as the clan leader, and she'd had me. Half our childhood, we'd fought with each other for fun or for some bogus excuse because we were siblings.

"She going to kill her?" Cricket asked against my shoulder as we looked on, helpless to avert her gaze.

Watching was the only way I could help Memphis. To be her support. As she used her strong limbs to flip Tina to the pavement and pin her with her mouth around her neck, I would know what my sister had to do to put a stop to the ways Tina had negatively impacted our lives.

Before I answered, Jack did. "Yes," he said while rubbing Astra's back. "That female cost me years of happiness while I watched the person I wanted to mate keep going back to a male I knew she didn't love. She tried to sell out her granddaughter, and now she must pay. And we will respect the position our ruler was put in to carry out the task."

I only studied them long enough to determine Astra felt the same way. She stayed in her mate's embrace, and I sensed nothing from them but grim acceptance. They wouldn't issue a vendetta against Memphis or me. Cricket wouldn't be hurt from the mess that was getting cleaned up today.

The sound of bones crunching made Cricket jump and gasp in my arms. She turned her face into my shoulder, unable to watch the gruesome end to Tina.

When the older woman was fully beheaded, Memphis stepped back, her resolve still strong. Her gaze was unwavering as she swung her head around to look at us. No one else could see the grief hiding under the anger but me. We had grown up with Tina. She wasn't our grandmother, but she'd been on the council serving our parents. Neither of us had sensed her animosity toward our family, and perhaps there had been no hatred but desperation that once she passed, her family would fade into obscurity, no longer serving the council and being mere townsfolk. For a proud female like Tina, the possibility was too hard to handle.

A car door slammed, and we all jerked our heads toward the sound. A low rumble emanated from Memphis.

My world dropped out from under me when a man's voice shouted, "What in God's name just happened?"

Vaughn.

Cricket

. . .

OH NO. It couldn't be. *No.*

"Vaughn?" I pushed away from Maverick but tangled the fingers of one hand into his to stay connected. I'd just witnessed the worst, most violent event I'd ever seen. I didn't want to be far from Maverick, even though this was the world he brought me into. I just watched a person get killed. A dragon. But so did my brother. I desperately wanted to be imagining all of today.

How could he be here? The drive would've taken too long. But as I stumbled off the sidewalk and between the parked cars along the curb, I saw my brother was indeed in Peridot Falls. His petrified and disbelieving gaze jerked from the mess on the pavement to me.

"Cricket? Are you okay?"

He ditched the unfamiliar car in the middle of the road and jogged toward me, looking completely normal yet so out of place in his crisp blue jeans and a forest-green cable-knit sweater. His loafers made soft clicking sounds on the pavement.

"For fuck's sake, another human." Memphis was out of breath and thoroughly disgusted. She'd shifted back and was naked, but that was the least distressing part of the moment.

My mouth hung open as I took in Vaughn and the body in the middle of the road. Tina was no longer a dragon. Her crumpled human form lay where the dragon had once been, and her head was completely severed. That detail remained unchanged. Shifters must return to their human form when they die, and if I had time to think about it, it would make sense. But I didn't. Because my brother was right here. And he'd seen something we couldn't explain. He now knew things that were dangerous for him to know—and he had no idea how much trouble he was in, and Memphis had just shown me exactly how she carried out punishments.

"Vaughn, what did you do? Why did you come here?" I couldn't wish him away. I wanted to be able to call him and tell him I was fine and to stay home. But I bet as soon as he'd heard me scream, he left Vegas to rush to my side, making me think he believed me.

He walked slowly toward me, his hands up, his gaze continuing to dart to Tina's body. The doctor inside of him couldn't help but verify he wouldn't be able to save her. Decapitation wasn't something a person—or shifters, it seemed—could come back from.

"I was worried about you." He beckoned me toward him like he was coaxing a scared dog. "Come with me, Cricket."

"No," I wailed, the trauma of what I'd witnessed catching up to me. "You've made it all worse. You're not supposed to be here. You weren't supposed to see..." I swept my hand toward the mess on the street.

"Dragons? That's what I saw." He was close to me now, but he stabbed a finger in the direction of the body. "That person was a dragon. And that naked woman?" He swung his arm toward Memphis. "Was also a dragon. I thought it was a play, or-or-or a movie, but she's"—he flung his arm back to point at Tina—"is dead. That's not a prop. I smell real blood."

He was pale, his body vibrating with terror. He tensed like he was going to wrestle me away from Maverick and sprint to the car that must be a rental.

"We can explain," Maverick said, sticking close to me as if he suspected the same.

"*Fuck*," growled Memphis as she stomped toward her clothing on the hood of one of the cars. "We've got a lot of explaining to do, all right. Right up to the point that we tell him he's going to—"

"Memphis." Maverick's tone made her snap her mouth shut and flap her shirt straight so she could put it on.

My vision was getting blurry. Tears swam in my eyes. "*No*. He can't... you can't... Maverick?" I broke into sobs. I was cocooned in Maverick's arms. I sensed my brother draw closer.

Vaughn beckoned me toward him. "Give her to me, Maverick."

"You're not going anywhere with her." The words rumbled from Maverick's chest. I liked his possessiveness, but I hated the situation.

"Cricket, you gotta come with me," Vaughn pleaded. "This town isn't safe for you."

I didn't disagree with him after the termination. But whether or not I went with him, he would call the police. He'd be on the phone now if he wasn't trying to talk himself out of the dragon part of what he saw and wasn't worried about me. I wasn't the one in danger right now.

I raised my head, my hands planted on Maverick's hard chest like he was the only thing that could keep me steady. "It's not me I'm worried about," I said to my brother. "It's you I'm scared of losing."

Memphis broke into the trio we made, fully dressed. "Take them into city hall," she told Maverick. "We need to deal with this."

I shook my head, the ends of my hair whipping my face. "You can't. You can't hurt him."

"Hurt me?" Confusion calmed Vaughn's urgency.

"No," Maverick said, his lips pressed thin. "We'll do this at my house. We'll talk there."

I fisted my hands into the material of Maverick's shirt. After what I just saw, I should know being out in the open didn't mean my brother was safe. But I didn't want to herd him into Maverick's house like a lamb going to slaughter. "You can't hurt him."

The anguish in Maverick's expression didn't make me feel better. "We need to go somewhere and talk. He needs to know what's on the line."

Hot tears tracked down my cheeks. Maverick wasn't giving me an unwavering affirmation he wouldn't hurt my brother—or that his sister wouldn't. "I was having a hard time moving away from Vaughn, but I can't lose him altogether. You have to help him."

"What's going on?" Vaughn threw his hands up in exasperation. "What the hell did I just see? And what are you talking about, Cricket?"

Maverick's sigh was full of regret. "We'll explain everything. But give my sister your phone and she'll drive you to my place."

"I can drive myself." The muscles in Vaughn's jaw jumped. "Why is no one mentioning the dead person on the street?"

"We'll take care of her," Astra said from the sidewalk. "The family will deal with her remains... and her dishonor."

Jack's nod was solemn.

"And who the hell are they?" Vaughn propped his hands on his hips.

Telling him would only complicate the story. "Hand your phone to Memphis and come with us." I let out a long exhale. "And I'll explain everything. I promise."

When Maverick gave his word, a heaviness hung in the air. My word was no different. If the only thing I could do for my brother was tell him the complete and honest truth, I would. But I wouldn't quit trying to save him any way I could.

Vaughn stared at me for a moment. He turned his attention to Memphis and raked his gaze down her fully clothed body. "And who's she?"

"Maverick's sister," I said. "And she's in charge of the town."

"Like the dragon mafia?" he asked sarcastically, then swallowed hard as if he couldn't believe he'd said such a thing. He swung his gaze to Tina's body and grimaced. "You killed her."

"I terminated her," Memphis said coolly. "There's a difference. Are you going to give your sister a chance to explain or keep prolonging this brand of special hell for us all? Give me your phone."

"I'm not giving up my fucking phone," he said through clenched teeth.

Memphis fisted her hands and my heart jumped into my throat. The last time she did that, someone died.

"Vaughn, please," I begged. "Just do it."

"Or what, Bug? She'll fight me for it?" His gaze drifted back to Tina and all the blood. "Fuck." He yanked it out of his pocket and tossed it like he didn't care where it landed.

Memphis snatched it out of the air and held the button down to shut it off. Annoyance crossed Vaughn's face. He would go where I went. I pried my hands loose. I had to make the first move. Then Vaughn would follow me, just like he did from Las Vegas when he'd tailed me right to his death.

FOURTEEN

CRICKET and her brother and Memphis were in my house. We were perched on my living room furniture, surrounded by downed blinds and half-painted walls. I'd been resisting the urge to shift into my dragon and rage through town since I'd heard Vaughn's voice.

This day had been a roller coaster, but the seats we were riding in had careened off the track. An epic fuckup I didn't see coming. One that would change our lives.

From the way Cricket trembled next to me, she understood the ramifications. She understood Vaughn had stumbled upon us and saw everything. In those cases, the outcome was nearly always tragic and supremely difficult for the clan ruler to get over. They had to carry out the termination. In this case, my sister would have to terminate my mate's brother.

Worst fucking scenario right there.

In a shaky voice, Cricket passed along all the information I had told her about our kind. I didn't have any experience revealing our secrets outside of Cricket and Vaughn but seeing us as dragons first certainly leaped over the initial obstacle of disbelief.

"That's all I know," Cricket finished quietly. Tears hadn't quit flowing down her face since she'd first started crying. I handed her tissues when all I wanted to do was kiss her fear away. But I couldn't. There was nothing I could do.

I had to figure out how to save her brother.

Memphis abruptly rose and paced the living room. Vaughn didn't budge from where he was perched on the end of a high-back chair. Astra had convinced me to buy that seat. Another whim I'd given in to, and after today, I knew why. The chair had been on my list to get rid of, but after learning she'd been under the influence of her grandma, I'd probably just keep it. As long as Cricket was okay with the decision.

As if Cricket would be okay being my mate after her brother was terminated.

Fuck. What a damn mess.

Vaughn tapped his fingertips together. Cricket had passed along the rules I'd informed her of, but she hadn't outright said what Vaughn was facing. The pieces were clicking together in his brain, judging from the tension radiating along his shoulders, the rigid set of his jaw, and the eerie stillness around him, except for that finger tap.

"So," he began. "If I'm interpreting what you said correctly, I have to be killed because I know about dragon shifters when I'm not marrying one of them?"

"We mate," I clarified. A small point among grander,

more serious ones but a clarification I needed to make. "It's a deeper connection than the vows humans say to each other."

Memphis snorted and continued to pace, her arms crossed over her chest. "And readily break."

I dipped my head. Another difference in our kinds that could cause issues. "When we make promises, we pay for not keeping them with our life."

Vaughn's gaze sharpened. "So when you said you wouldn't hurt my sister?"

Memphis pinned a glare on me. I'd make the same vow over and over again. I'd found another loophole, and I detested it. Vaughn's death would hurt Cricket more than anything, but I was only indirectly responsible, and therefore my promise still held. What a shitty thought.

"She won't suffer for me knowing…" He twirled his finger in the air like he was encompassing all of the shifter world in one gesture.

She sniffled. "I'm going to suffer." I handed her another tissue. I continued to rub her back, but any more bad news and I'd wear a hole through her shirt.

"I don't get it." The tapping quit, but he pressed his fingertips together until his knuckles turned white. "Why can't I just promise not to tell anyone? I keep important information to myself as part of my job every damn day. I talk to parents knowing full well their child doesn't have a chance of surviving, but I still cover treatment options."

The steady thunk of Memphis's boots pounded on the floor. "All it takes is one person to break their word. And as I said, humans are piss poor at keeping their promises."

He shot her a glare. "I'm not just any human."

She flashed an annoyed smile. "The only part of that sentence I care about is that you're human."

He shook his head like he was ignoring what she said. If he wanted to anger Memphis in a way she wouldn't care if she had to kill him or not, he was doing a good job. Memphis doled out attitude; she hated receiving it. "And if I moved to Peridot Falls? Lived among you in this shifter cult? Is that sufficient?"

I opened my mouth to answer, but Memphis beat me to it. "Our laws have been our laws for centuries. No human can reside within our clan's city limits unless they are a mate. Then they are invested in the secret, and they've seen what happens to those who break our laws. Just like your sister is probably wondering what the hell she got into."

Cricket cringed against me. Dammit, Memphis. But she was likely right. I couldn't believe Cricket hadn't tried to run at the first sign of bloodshed. Her worry for her brother kept her with me. She was relying on me to fix this, and I couldn't fail her.

Vaughn's annoyance was tipped with growing desperation. "Surely you don't kick human children out who don't get the shifter trait?"

"The shifter side is always dominant," I said before Memphis answered in a harsh way that upset him more. The more riled Vaughn was, the more disturbed Cricket would get.

"There's got to be a way." Vaughn's tone made it easy to picture him as an arrogant doctor striding through the halls of the hospital. "I refuse to believe that after centuries"—he shot another annoyed look toward Memphis—"your people haven't thought of a way to prevent the murder of innocent humans."

"As a doctor," Memphis said, irritation ripe in her voice, "you should understand nothing's one hundred percent. We have a boatload of preventative measures that you blew right through."

"It's not Vaughn's fault," Cricket said hotly, just as disgruntled with my sister as Vaughn. "He was worried about me."

"He didn't believe you," Memphis countered. "And he acted impulsively."

I held up my hands. "Okay, our emotions are justifiably riding high. Memphis, if I give you my word that Vaughn isn't going anywhere, will you give us some time to talk?"

So much tension radiated from my sister. She should've been vibrating. She didn't want to terminate Vaughn any more than we wanted her to. "I want *his* promise he isn't going to leave. *His* word, since he thinks that should mean so much coming from a human."

The man practically rolled his eyes. Did he have a death wish, or did he figure he was far enough in the grave he'd never get out? "Like it would do any good." Some of his anger drained away. "I'm not leaving my sister with creatures who'd rather spill blood than have a decent conversation."

Memphis spun on him. "You weren't here for the conversation. You weren't here for the fifteen years that female fucked around in my brother's life and the lives of others in my clan. You weren't here when she wanted to terminate our other brother. You aren't the one who has to dole out the punishment and take shit from everyone who thinks they could've done better."

He only rewarded her impassioned speech with a steady glower.

I had to get them separated, or he was going to keep antagonizing her. I didn't trust his word, not where his sister was concerned. He'd admitted to lying for what he thought was the greater good. If he thought Cricket was miserable or in danger, he wasn't beneath attempting to abduct her and escape. My respect for him grew. His protectiveness had bitten all of us in the ass, but it was for my mate, and for that, I struggled to be upset with him.

"I'll watch over them. Nothing's going to happen to anyone until we examine this issue from all sides. Right, Memphis?"

She ignored me and finally stopped pacing to face Vaughn. "You try to leave, I will find you. If you try to call anyone, write a letter, or use Morse code to tell anyone about us, I'll take your head so fast you won't have a chance to roll your eyes again."

Cricket let out a startled gasp that dissolved into a sob.

I wrapped my arms around her and cradled her to my chest. "Christ, Memphis. Did you have to?"

The glare she turned on me brimmed with rage and frustration. "Yes," she hissed. "You, of all people, know exactly what I have to do. So, *I'm sorry* if I made your mate cry." She spun on a heel and stomped out of the house.

Without Memphis's fiery presence, the air in the room felt lighter, but it was only the difference between a blistering frying pan and a vat of hot grease.

I pinched the bridge of my nose. "Cricket, I'm so sorry. If I knew this would happen, I would've forced myself to walk away from you that night."

Her body shook harder. "It's not fair. He was only worried about me."

"No, it isn't fair." Our laws were meant to protect. My gaze connected with Vaughn's.

His jaw was clenched, and anguish was written over his expression. "You really don't think there's a way out? I'm just gonna be gone, and my patients are going to be left floundering? Do you plan to feed the hospital some bullshit line about how I went hiking and was found at the bottom of some trail without my head?"

A full-bodied spasm racked Cricket. "Stop it, Vaughn. I don't know who's worse, you or Memphis."

"Now you're just being hateful," Vaughn said, and I almost laughed. The absurdity of his comment with the gravity of the situation was just wrong.

Gravity won out. "Memphis is in a hard spot. The fight you saw was her doing her job, and the dead female was someone we had grown up respecting, an elder Memphis had worked with for years that we learned had betrayed all of us. She's had a shit day, and it's not looking to end anytime soon."

Vaughn's granite expression didn't waver. "You'll have to excuse me if I don't empathize with the woman who's supposed to murder me."

Cricket abruptly sat up. She pushed the heels of her hands against her eyes. "Maverick, can you give me and Vaughn some space to talk?"

Tiny shards of hurt stabbed me in the chest. She and I had a connection, but to Vaughn, I was the guy who took his sister away and plopped her in the middle of violent people. He hadn't seen how, for the most part, we live just like humans. "Of course."

"Where you won't be able to hear us?" She put her hand on my knee, her expression bleak. "I'd like to speak freely without worrying about hurting your feelings. But with your hearing, if you're in the house..."

I'd be in on the entire conversation. "I'll be outside."

I gave her a quick kiss on the temple. Her flinch was slight but noticeable. I detested that was her reaction to me. We should be over the moon happy instead of planning for her brother's death.

~

CRICKET

"I'M SO SORRY." Nothing I said was good enough. No words could make up for the trouble my actions had gotten him into. There was no way to make this complicated mess easy.

Vaughn slumped in the chair, pressing the fingers of one hand to his temples. "I can't believe what I saw. But I saw it, and I can't deny it. And now I can't believe that my life is on the line because—fucking *dragons*."

"Maverick and Memphis will figure something out. They have to."

Vaughn gave me a doubtful look, but I shook my head and continued. "They have to. There's no way I can live in a town that's willing to kill you. There's no way."

"Neither of them seems to be inclined to come up with a solution."

"We need time. That's all." I was forcing my confidence, but the only other choice was acceptance, and I couldn't do it. I couldn't accept that my sister-in-law would have to terminate my brother. I couldn't accept that the person I fell in love with would throw his hands up in the air and not do anything.

"Time." Vaughn huffed out a laugh. "There's never enough time." His tone grew increasingly bitter. "Not enough time with our parents. Not enough time to teach you everything you need to know about the world while I was going to school. Not enough time to research diseases and save my patients. Not enough time to get away from work and get here to make sure you're okay. Never any damn time."

This was my first glimpse into the stress my brother had been under since our parents had died. Before that, it'd been normal pressure. School, part-time job, socializing. Then he'd had to raise me, and now he was pushing forty with no family of his own, a sense of failure for every patient he couldn't save, and there was an axe poised above his neck, waiting for the final decision to be made.

"I'm going to help you," I said as if speaking it made it so.

He dropped his hand to hang off the arm of the chair. Fatigue hung off him like a dark shroud, only visible when you cared enough to look. And I'd been so wrapped up in myself over the last several years—well, always—to notice.

I could see it in his expression. Defeat. He felt like he had failed everyone. Our parents, me, his patients, and maybe himself. My big, strong brother was tired and empty. He'd given everything to those around him and the cost was due. The price was everything.

More tears tracked down my cheeks, but I wasn't giving up. I would be strong for him. "This isn't over. Between all of us, we can figure something out."

His eyelids drifted shut. "Dragons." After a few heart-beats, he flipped his eyes open and pinned me with his hazel gaze. "I've seen things in my career, shit I couldn't explain. Kids would die with no explanation. Everything would be going well, and then they were gone. And some children that were not only knocking on death's door, but pushing their way through, pulled back from the brink. Complete recovery. I understood there were forces out there beyond me, beyond all medicine, and that there was only so much I could do as a human physician. But goddamn dragons?"

"It blows my mind. They've been around forever, and we've never known."

His lips took on a scornful twist. "Because they slaughter anyone who finds out."

The tears kept coming. "I'm not losing you, Vaughn."

He abruptly sat forward, and I flinched. His tone was as hard as his gaze. "You won't do anything to put yourself at risk."

"I'm not just standing by while they decide there's nothing they can do." It wouldn't happen. I couldn't allow it. I was in a new world, as powerless as a newborn baby, but there had to be something I could do.

"I watched that woman—that thing—rip another dragon's head off. You cannot let them hurt you." He shook his head, shadows covering his face. "If I thought there was somewhere we could go and they couldn't find you, we'd take off this instant. But I don't know enough about them."

"If we both run, there'll be two termination orders." I wasn't yet mated to Maverick, and I doubted our marriage vows would go far if I tried to flee. I'd lose the tenuous trust of the shifters I'd met, and I'd lose my chance with any others.

My chest ached at the thought. I didn't want to leave Maverick, but I didn't want to stay at the cost of my brother. A fracture was breaking my heart in two.

How much would I be punished if I helped my brother run away? I didn't know when the change from figuring it all out to escape took place, but my mind wasn't exactly functioning smoothly today. "We need to figure out how to get you out of here."

He shook his head again. "I'm not living a life on the run. I've worked too damn hard for what I have to leave it all behind. If that woman thinks she's gonna chop through my neck like—" He clenched his jaw, his eyes haunted. "She just..."

"Yeah, it was gruesome." It didn't seem real. Like I watched a 3D movie. But the decapitated human body? That would stay with me. My brother had seen enough in his time as a doctor, but I was an accounts manager who never watched horror flicks. Seeing Tina like that was the first time I'd questioned living with Maverick. I'd heard what Tina had done and was told stories of how it affected the ones involved, but for such a severe punishment? It was extreme.

"I can't leave you here with killers, Cricket."

I thought of raising a family in Peridot Falls. Memphis would be my children's aunt. Briony would be another aunt, and Levi, their uncle, but they didn't have the same type of responsibility and clan expectations Memphis did. What if my kids messed up and needed to be terminated?

What if my kids needed protection, and they had an aunt who was willing to kill to do it?

The answer to one question was a nightmare, and the answer to the other made me feel a little messed up. This wasn't the world I had grown up in.

"You can't be considering staying with him?" Disbelief drowned his words. "You've only known him for a week."

"I knew Peterson for years, and he turned out to be a different man than I thought he was."

"Peterson is a sleaze, but he's not a killer."

I ground my teeth. "Neither is Maverick."

"Do you know that, Bug?"

No, I didn't. But he was so caring, about me, about his people, I knew if he did take a life, it was for an honorable reason. The same could be said for his sister. She had taken no joy in what she did.

"I'm torn," I said truthfully. "But if I had to set a hard limit, it would be your death." I shrugged. That was the best I could do. I'd give Maverick everything, but I wouldn't give up on my brother.

CHAPTER
FIFTEEN

averick

I PACED the edge of the yard, far enough away from the house I couldn't hear Cricket and Vaughn talk. Were they plotting Vaughn's escape? Was Cricket pleading with her brother to help her get away from me? I shoved a hand through my hair and held my phone to my ear.

Memphis was likely busy with the fallout of Tina's termination. The council would demand answers, the rest of the townsfolk would want in an official statement, and then there was the cleanup. In the middle of goddamn town. Right in front of my mate. Out in the open, where anyone driving through could see, and it happened at the only time we had an unsuspecting human coasting through town.

Fuck, I couldn't let Vaughn take the fall for this. He was a pediatrician. A caring brother. He'd done nothing but help people for his entire adult life. Shifters couldn't be the ones to take him from the world. And I couldn't be involved in taking him away from Cricket.

It had chewed me up enough at the thought she'd have to occasionally lie to him and keep her distance. But terminating him?

As soon as I left the house, I had wanted to call Memphis, but I had called Levi instead. I needed someone who knew the whole story, who understood the constraints of being in the ruling family, but who wasn't Memphis.

"There's got to be a way," Levi said, echoing my thoughts.

"Memphis is seeing pretty damn black and white right now."

"I can't blame her. Taking out Tina is going to be hard on her."

Another thread of conflict tingled in my chest. There'd been a time in my life when Tina had been family. Both Memphis and I had grown up thinking of her as an aunt. Levi was younger than us and wasn't as close to her, but he'd witnessed the connection.

"We've got to figure out how to save Cricket's brother. She's not going to stay with me if something happens to him." It didn't matter how new our relationship was, the results would be the same whether we'd been together a week or twenty years. Being associated with the death of her only relative was a deal breaker.

"Memphis isn't there right now, with her teeth bared, ready to tear him apart, is she?"

"No." A large part of me had worried earlier how soon she'd insist on carrying out the termination. A quick end to get it over with and begin healing. But she'd been reeling from the fight, and I hoped she also wanted time to figure out how to extract us from the mess we found ourselves in.

"There's that. Let me talk to her."

He wasn't as close to her as I was. "I should—"

"You're too attached to this. She's going to think you only care about your mate and not her."

I snapped my mouth shut. I cared about them both, but while I'd only known Cricket for a matter of days, my mate took priority.

"I'll talk to her. If she's willing to explore any option we can think of, I'll help her figure that shit out. But she saved my ass when the council wanted me gone. I don't believe she's going to hurt Cricket's brother if she can avoid it."

Levi's logic loosened the knot behind my sternum. "Tell her..." Was I really going to lay out an ultimatum? Yes, because I couldn't live with myself if I shattered Cricket's world. "Tell her if we can't get out of the termination order, I'm taking Vaughn's place."

"Dammit, Maverick. This is messed up enough as it is."

"Those are my terms. Nothing happens to him."

He made a disgusted sound. "They'll never let a human roam around who knows about us and isn't a mate."

"I heard Silver clan was willing to allow it when Deacon gave himself up for Ava."

Levi went quiet for a moment. "I thought that was just a rumor."

"A true one." I had filed the knowledge away, not knowing I would end up using it someday.

"Memphis is going to shit all over the messenger, but yeah, I'll tell her."

"I appreciate it. I'll make sure Vaughn and Cricket stay at my place, and we'll wait to hear what she says."

"Got it." Levi hung up, and I dropped my arm by my side, phone clutched in my hand. A sense of peace settled over me. Nothing was going to happen to Vaughn. I wouldn't allow it. But in the end, I was asking Memphis to do the unthinkable.

And I'd hope she'd eventually see that my sacrifice was saving two innocent people.

THE REST of the day stretched out with one long second ticking after another. Cricket was curled up in the corner of the couch, Vaughn reclined in the chair, but he stared at the ceiling, and I sat at the other end of the couch with my hand resting on Cricket's legs. She wasn't in a cuddly mood, but I needed to touch her. Instinctively, I knew she wouldn't want me to heal her headache. My fingers twitched to do it, but I had to be satisfied seeing after her in other ways. No one had an appetite, but I'd encouraged each of them to drink some water.

Not exactly Florence Nightingale shit, but it was something.

Cricket swung her legs down and sat up. A heavy sigh escaped her lips. "I know we asked for time, but this is driving all of us crazy."

"It's the waiting game. But it's a good sign." Both of their gazes lifted to me. "Levi said he'd talk to Memphis, and the council hasn't appeared on my lawn. So there's hope."

Her gaze brightened. "You really think we can get out of this?"

Not unscathed. But I wasn't going to tell her that. "We all refuse to believe there aren't any other options." I spread my hands apart. "So that must mean we feel like there's something else we can do."

Just as a heavy weight seemed to flow off her shoulders, my phone rang. They stared at me, and I held in my groan. I dug the phone out of my pocket and inwardly winced. Memphis. "Yeah?"

"Get your ass to city hall and bring the other two with you."

"Did you—"

She hung up.

I met Cricket's questioning gaze and remembered she couldn't hear as well as shifters. "Memphis needs us to come to city hall."

Moisture shimmered in Cricket's eyes. I moved to hold her, but she flinched backward. My heart dropped. This felt like the beginning of the end.

Vaughn's glare rested on me. "That's it? She just told us to show up with no answers about who gets to live and who has to die?"

"She doesn't owe us an explanation. She's in charge." He needed to know how it worked around here. I couldn't make excuses for Memphis when our laws were there for a reason. She held the power she did for a reason.

Cricket sniffled and swiped her hands over her cheeks. "Are we leading him to his death?"

"I'm not going to let Vaughn die," I said quietly. She narrowed her eyes at me, and I lifted a shoulder. "I'll do everything in my power to keep that from happening."

"Would you get hurt instead?" she asked, alarm in her gaze.

I rose and held my hand out to her. "We need to get going. We need to know their answer before we can counter."

Vaughn stood. "I thought there was no negotiation."

"Maybe not," was all I could offer.

His lips thinned, and he marched out the door. Cricket and I watched him go.

"I'm scared, Maverick."

"I know."

She let me put my arm around her and lead her out the door. I wasn't sure if Vaughn had stormed out of the house and kept on going, but he was sitting in the back seat of my pickup. The drive to city hall was over in a blink. The street in front of city hall was cleared of cars. Someone had managed to get all the blood off the pavement after Tina's body was removed. But it was the sight of Memphis, Levi, Briony, and the remaining three members of the council that made the acid levels in my gut churn.

I got out and was going around to be with Cricket when she climbed out of the pickup, but Memphis stomped across the road.

"What is it with you?" Her shout filled the silent street. "You keep putting yourself in the place of these two, thinking I can kill you!"

She continued charging toward me and shoved me with both hands. I wasn't ready for this type of confrontation, and I stumbled backward, but I wouldn't have stopped her anyway. I could take her anger. She needed to vent.

"Memphis, you've gotta understand—"

"I understand you're a selfless bastard who puts me in the worst possible position to save a couple of innocent dumbasses."

Vaughn's snide reply didn't help. "If you're going to kill me, I can do without the name-calling."

Cricket peeked from behind him. Vaughn was doing the same thing I would've, trying to put himself between her and possible danger.

Memphis rounded on him, her face a mask of rage. "Oh, but I won't be terminating you. Maverick demanded to be put in your place."

Cricket's gasp silenced us all. "*No*. You can't. You can't hurt him."

Memphis rounded on Cricket, and I tensed, prepared to jump between the two. Would my sister take her ire out on Cricket?

"No, I can't!" she yelled. "That's why your brother and I are going to have to get mated."

Loaded silence descended on all of us.

Several seconds went by before Danielle sputtered, "Mate?"

"I'm confused," Vaughn said.

Cricket elbowed past Vaughn, hope radiating through her entire body and her grateful gaze on Memphis. "You would do that?"

My feet rooted in place. My sister, who never dated, was willing to mate a man she had just met to save me? Not only was she sparing our lives but also our anguish.

"Memphis," I breathed. "Are you sure?"

It was the perfect answer. For me and Cricket. But for Vaughn and Memphis? Vaughn would be alive, but he'd have to leave everything he knew, and Memphis would be in a pairing she didn't want.

Her brow wrinkled, and Memphis shoved her hands in the air. "What choice have you given me?" She flicked her finger back and forth between her and Vaughn. "He can't know about our kind unless he's one of our mates. I can't exactly terminate him without hurting my brother and the love of his life. Not very sister-in-law of me. And I don't exactly like having innocent lives on my conscience. I'm definitely not killing either of my brothers, and I don't fucking care what either of you does. I'm never hurting either one of you."

She finished with a growl, and her frustration emanated into me. The last several months had taken a toll. The threat to Levi. Then me.

Confusion marred Vaughn's brow. "So me and her?" he asked Cricket.

Memphis grimaced. "Yes."

Cricket pressed her fingers against her lips. I was across from her, the four of us were like the points of the compass.

"I can't believe it," she said around her fingertips. "I can't believe it, but yes. You two and you'd have to move here."

"It's... not the worst plan in the world," I finally said.

"You're not the one mating some human you just met," Memphis growled.

I sort of was, but her disgruntlement was the sweetest sound to my ears. Did I want my sister to be with a guy she didn't really know? No, but it was far better than leaving her with another death or two on her conscience.

I barely knew Vaughn, but I knew enough. He was a good man. A guy who took his obligation seriously and looked after everyone in his life. If I had to choose traits for my sister's mate, they would be at the top. Whether they would learn to like each other, I didn't know. No one did, but that was up to them.

Danielle toddled across the street. She was probably still shaken from this morning. "It would behoove us to do both ceremonies as soon as possible. Our unrest will soon reach the other clans, and none of us care to have the Silvers in our business."

The muscles in Memphis's jaw jumped. The Silvers were respected, but rulers didn't like other rulers in their business. "If we're already mated by the time the other clans hear about our drama, it'll look better, and the Silvers will be less likely to interfere."

Vaughn backed up a step. "Get married? Now?"

"Oh, big guy," Memphis said, her tone full of sass. "This is so much more than marrying. Hope you weren't dating anyone in Vegas. Because you're mine now."

Their expressions matched, so different than Cricket's hopeful optimism.

Vaughn swung his head toward his sister. "Is she serious? I marry her, and we're all free to just do our thing?"

"Yes," Cricket said softly. "It's extremely generous of Memphis."

Vaughn's gaze collided with Memphis's challenging one. My sister wasn't going to make it easy on him.

"I'm not moving." He crossed his arms over his chest.

Danielle raised a finger. "While others can mate out of necessity and have an otherwise open relationship, you will be mated to our ruler, which means... uh... which means you will need to attempt to procreate."

Memphis blanched, and Vaughn's eyes flared.

"Procreate," he echoed.

Danielle nodded. I wanted to be upset on my sister's

behalf, but the relief overpowered me. A huge grin spread on my face and I met Cricket's gaze. She was stunned, but her lips pulled into a wide smile. "This is utterly ridiculous," she said.

"I have to move?" Vaughn's indignant question broke between us. "And have kids with you?"

"Don't flatter yourself, big guy. I'm not looking forward to it any more than you are." Memphis spun on a heel and marched back across the street. A nervous Danielle fluttered after her.

Briony was tucked into Levi's side, shaking her head. But the deep satisfaction in Levi's eyes told me he'd been the one to come up with the idea.

I gave him a nod, and he returned it. I crossed to Cricket, swooped her in my arms, and picked her up. "I'm so sorry, but this is the best we could ask for."

"Your sister's going to hate me. But at least she won't be faced with hurting you or Vaughn."

I had to trust they'd work it out, just like Cricket and I had.

~

CRICKET

THE DAY HAD FINALLY COME. What had only been a matter of weeks had stretched on forever. While I'd happily anticipated the day I could be bonded to Maverick and officially begin my new life in Peridot Falls, my brother had barely spoken to me. He'd returned the rental car, flown back to Vegas, quit his job, and moved out of his condo.

Maverick and I had driven back to Las Vegas so I could pack what I was bringing to Minnesota with me and give away or sell the rest. As soon as we were done and the place was up for sale, we loaded up and returned to Peridot Falls. My brother had stayed in Vegas until the last minute, arriving back in town hours before the ceremony was ready to begin.

As for Memphis, it was business as usual, at least to me. Maverick said she was moodier, her answers curt, and she had holed up in her office a lot more than usual. Vaughn's hybrid SUV and the U-Haul were parked outside of Memphis's ranch-style home. Maverick said she had an extra bedroom, and I was certain that was where Vaughn would stay.

As for the procreation... not my business.

My sympathy for my brother and Memphis spilled over, but not enough for me to truly regret what happened. Maverick wouldn't have to live with the guilt, and neither would I. All of it seems selfish, but compared to how everything could've turned out, I couldn't bring myself to dwell on it. My brother was safe, and while I hated he was forced to live in the same town I had moved to, I selfishly got to have him around me. Alive. That part was the most important. And Memphis was safe from the birthday deadline. It wasn't for a few years, but Maverick didn't have to tell me he'd already been worried.

Maybe Vaughn and Memphis would find their own nebulous happiness.

Maverick and I mated first, hoping to ease the way for our siblings. Levi and Briony were witnesses, and we had crowded into city hall's meeting room with Danielle and the other two council members. I stood next to them, with my arms wrapped around Maverick as they finished completing their vows to each other. There was something about the ceremony that I didn't recall from our wedding. I might've had a few drinks then, and I was absolutely sober now, but I felt closer to Maverick than ever. Sure, we were rounding out a month of knowing each other, but our spark had flamed into a wildfire almost immediately. Our love for each other only continued to grow as we finished painting the walls of the house, picked new blinds, and installed cabinets. Home renovations could drive other couples apart, but we were having fun together.

As I watched Vaughn participate in his bonding ceremony to Memphis, I wanted the same for him. But all signs pointed to no. His mouth was set in a troubled line and he'd folded his arms over his chest, staring at the ground. No part of him touched Memphis, who was standing next to him with her hands in her back pockets and one knee cocked to the side like she needed to hear the end before she charged back to her office.

Danielle wrapped up, a small, tentative smile on her face.

"That's it," Memphis announced like she'd wrapped up a speech and wanted all of us to go away.

A couple of females I was told who worked at the bank stood with them and Honor I had gotten to know from the diner. Her painting hung above our bed.

Levi gave one clap, and it appeared Briony was holding her breath. "Congratulations. It's done." Levi managed to properly sum some things up. Congratulations for me and Maverick. *It's done* for Vaughn and Memphis.

Vaughn ignored his new mate and spoke to me. "If you'll excuse me, I've got work to do."

He left the meeting room and went in one direction toward the exit, and Memphis veered the other way to her office. At first glance, those two were polar opposites, but they were more alike than I first thought. Mostly in that they both hid in their work. Would either of them be able to tear the other away from duties and obligations, or would they double down to escape each other? There was more to life, and I wanted my brother to know it as much as Maverick wanted his sister to experience it.

Briony's expression was pleasant, albeit cautious, as she made conversation. "He was able to work remotely?"

I nodded. "He'll be working with a hospital in Minneapolis. He'll see patients online and travel to the city a few times a month for in-office visits."

"The best of both worlds?" Briony's question would've been a plain statement had Vaughn acted like he wanted to be here. But we all knew he had no choice, no one more acutely than him and Memphis.

"We can hope," was all I said.

Maverick's thumb massaged a small circle on my upper arm as if he knew what I was thinking. "Honor has a special meal for us at the diner, complete with Briony's celebratory scones."

Briony nodded and Levi said, "I left a half dozen in Memphis's office. I didn't think she'd stick around. Briony and I will meet you at the diner." He led his mate out. The others filtered out behind them.

Maverick and I were alone in the meeting room. He brought my hand to his lips and feathered a kiss over the peridot stone set into the gold band from our wedding. His impressive hoard was filled with all kinds of jewels, but I was partial to peridot. It reminded me of his eyes.

I gave him a weary smile. "A little bittersweet with our happy day."

"It's up to those two to figure it out. But Memphis might need a kick in the ass."

"I'll leave that up to you." I doubted I could reach Memphis's ass. "But maybe it's time I push my brother out of his comfort zone."

"Oh, I think he's there."

I shook my head. "No. He has a job. He's going to bury himself in it."

Maverick's gaze strayed to the door. "I feel terrible, but I'm also really happy right now, but they'll figure it out. And they're stubborn enough to make us want to suffer in our guilt."

"Stubborn is an understatement when it comes to Vaughn. I hope he's as happy here as I am." I hadn't fought off a single headache since the drama right after my arrival. A town full of shifters with sensitive hearing was blissfully quiet. I tucked myself into his side. "Let's go celebrate... mate."

"Did you know it's tradition to steal a brand-new mate away for a quick fuck during the reception?"

I feigned surprise as we walked out of the room together. "Are you sure that's a thing, or are you just making it up?"

"I've been to a few mating ceremonies, and each time the couple disappears for a while."

Grinning, I charged out the door with him and toward the rest of our lives. "Well, I definitely don't want to break tradition."

———

. . .

FIND out if Vaughn gets over his shock and comes around to the idea of being a dragon shifter's mate in The Dragon's Affirmation.

FOR NEW RELEASE UPDATES, chapter sneak peeks, and exclusive quarterly short stories, sign up for Marie's newsletter and receive my first wolf shifter story FREE.

About the Author

Marie Johnston writes paranormal and contemporary romance and has collected several awards in both genres. Before she was a writer, she was a microbiologist. Depending on the situation, she can be oddly unconcerned about germs or weirdly phobic. She's also a licensed medical technician and has worked as a public health microbiologist and as a lab tech in hospital and clinic labs. Marie's been a volunteer EMT, a college instructor, a security guard, a phlebotomist, a hotel clerk, and a coffee pourer in a bingo hall. All fodder for a writer!! She has four kids, an old cat, and a puppy that's bigger than half her kids.

mariejohnstonwriter.com

Follow me:

Also by Marie Johnston

Silver Dragon Shifter Brothers

The Dragon's Oath

The Dragon's Promise

The Dragon's Vow

Jade Dragon Shifter Brothers

The Dragon's Pledge

The Dragon's Bond

Peridot Dragon Shifter Brothers

The Dragon's Word

The Dragon's Dedication

The Dragon's Affirmation

www.ingramcontent.com/pod-product-compliance
Lightning Source LLC
Chambersburg PA
CBHW061446210726
48287CB00007B/2384